LOST IN
THE PAST

Books by
Jenny Elaine

Rose of Savannah Series

The Healing Rose of Savannah
The Whispering Shadows of Savannah

A Shady Pines Mystery Series

Secrets from the Past
Lost in the Past
Storms of the Past

A SHADY PINES MYSTERY – BOOK 2

LOST IN THE PAST

JENNY ELAINE

ISBN: 979-8-9853661-1-2

PROLOGUE

25 YEARS EARLIER

She paced around the small, cramped living room, wringing her hands nervously as fear clutched at her spine. Ever since her three students had disappeared, she'd had a feeling something terrible had happened, and today she'd accidentally stumbled upon the truth. *I've got to tell someone,* she thought, anxiety causing her fingers to tremble. *But who would believe me? I have no proof.*

Glancing over at the little Winnie the Pooh teddy bear she'd just bought for her daughter, she began to cry. They were all alone here and could both be killed if she told the truth. She couldn't risk her daughter's life. She had to get out of here.

After throwing a few things into a small suitcase, she put her daughter to bed and took a quick shower. She'd decided to leave first thing in the morning, and there were still quite a few things she needed to get done before bed. *How do you think you're going to get any sleep after what you've discovered?* She thought as she stepped from the shower and slipped into a robe. She'd suspected this for a while, and now that she knew the truth, it was eating her up inside.

She'd just pulled her hair into a ponytail when a faint creak in her bedroom caught her attention. Catching her breath, she switched off the bathroom light and pressed her back against the wall, her heart pounding as she waited.

The bathroom door opened slowly, and she could hear the sound of soft, even breaths as a shadow fell upon the floor. Had her daughter possibly climbed out of her crib? Should she call out, instead of hovering against the far wall like a scared animal? Before she could gather her thoughts, the overhead light clicked on and she saw the person she feared the most standing in the doorway with a gun.

"Going somewhere?" the intruder asked, holding up the little travel bag she'd left lying on the bed.

"N-no," she stammered, the pounding of her heart so loud she could barely hear the sound of her own voice.

"I don't believe you, especially since I know you overheard my conversation earlier today. Although you were never on my list, it seems that I'll have to get rid of you now, too."

"Please, just leave me alone," she begged, her voice almost a whisper. "I-I won't tell anyone."

With a cynical grin, the gun was raised as a snide voice hissed, "I still don't believe you."

She lunged to the right just as the gun fired, the bullet barely missing her head. Grabbing a can of disinfectant, she blindly sprayed the chemical in the direction of the door and a scream of pain immediately met her ears. Her assailant stumbled backward, giving her a split second to push by and race from the room.

She ran into her daughter's bedroom and had just turned on the light when she heard the pounding of footsteps coming down the hall after her. Glancing wildly around for another weapon, her eyes landed on a nearby giraffe figurine that was solid brass, and she yanked it from its resting place just as the door was flung open.

Pressing her back against the wall beside the door, she trembled from head to toe as the nose of the gun peaked around the corner.

"I know you're in here," the evil voice called out and, taking her chance, she swung the figurine and knocked the gun to the floor with a *crack.*

The next few seconds were a blur. As she tried to make a lunge toward the gun, her assailant quickly grabbed her by the hair and yanked her backward. Her neck snapping painfully, stars floated before her eyes just as two cold hands wrapped around her throat.

"Mommy!"

Her daughter had awakened, and from the corner of her eye, she could see her standing up in her crib, clutching the little Winnie the Pooh bear as she cried.

Her motherly instincts kicking in, she felt a rush of adrenaline flood over her and began to fight back with renewed strength. The figurine was still clutched in her hand, and she swung it upward as hard as she could until it met with her assailant's temple. She felt the icy hands loosen and heard a loud *thump* as the body hit the floor.

Stumbling back, she stared in horror at the blood that oozed onto the carpet. Had she just killed a person, or would those hate-filled eyes pop open at any second?

When a moan was suddenly uttered, she knew it was only a matter of minutes until the intruder regained total consciousness.

Her heart kicking into overdrive, she grabbed her sobbing daughter, threw on her clothes, and ran toward the front of the house. *Where is my purse?* she thought as she hurried into the kitchen, her eyes searching frantically for the small black handbag. She expected to hear the sound of footsteps at any moment; she needed to hurry, but couldn't get away without her car keys. Finally, her eyes landed on the bag, and with a sigh of relief, she grabbed it and ran outside to her car.

"M-mommy?"

Her little girl clung to her blouse as she buckled her into the car seat with quick, jerky movements. Tears stained her little cheeks, and her beautiful eyes were wide with fear.

"It's going to be okay, sweetie," she said, kissing her on the forehead as she gently pried her blouse from her daughter's fingers.

Closing the car door, she jumped into the

driver's seat and fumbled with the keys, a moan of frustration passing from her lips when they fell at her feet with a clatter. Her heart pounding as she grasped along the floor in search of the keys, she wondered how much longer she had before the front door was thrown open and she felt the cool barrel of a gun pressing against her temple. She'd just managed to grab the keys and crank the car when she saw a shadow moving along the living room windows. With a catch of her breath, she quickly slammed the car into reverse, the tires squealing as she backed out onto the road and took off.

She continually checked the rearview mirror, but knew that even if she was being followed, she wouldn't see any headlights because they wouldn't be turned on. The night was dark, and her mind spun in a thousand different directions as she tried to figure out what to do.

"I scared, Mommy."

Her little girl's voice suddenly broke the silence in the car, and her heart caught in her throat.

"Don't be scared, honey," she said, trying to soothe the fear and uncertainty she heard in her daughter's voice. "Mommy will take care of you."

I've got to make sure she's safe, she thought, tears filling her eyes as she realized with sickening certainty that this nightmare wouldn't stop until they were both found and killed. Her daughter was only three, but she could still talk and tell the police what she'd witnessed that night, and she knew how dangerous that was for her.

Seeing the sign up ahead that read *Cloud Haven*, she made a last-minute decision and turned toward the small, familiar town. As she drove, she wondered if she was doing the right thing. How could she leave her child, not knowing if she'd ever see her again? Glancing over her shoulder to watch as her sweet baby dozed back off to sleep, her little arms still clutching her teddy bear, she knew that making certain her life would be protected was the most important thing right now. ***I'll make sure she's safe, and then I'll go to the police,*** she told herself. ***I have to tell what I know; it's the only way this madness will ever end.***

Parking the car just outside of town under a thick grove of trees, she grabbed her daughter and hurried down the long, quiet road, the clicking of her shoes against the pavement the only sound in the lonely night. As she clutched her little girl tighter in her arms, she glanced fearfully over her shoulder, her eyes searching the darkness. She expected to see a shadow leaping out at them any minute, but she had to get her daughter to safety before it was too late. She ***had*** to.

She entered the quiet, sleeping town and glanced up ahead, the cathedral's steeple rising up above the tops of the buildings like a large beacon against an indigo sky. She quickened her steps, her lungs screaming for air.

"What happening, Mommy?" her little girl asked, having been awakened once again when her mother snatched her from the car seat.

"We're going to see Father Andrews," she said, trying to force a bit of cheerfulness into her whispered voice. "You remember him, don't you, honey?"

She knew her daughter was confused, but how could she possibly explain what was happening to a three-year-old? Perhaps when all of this was over and they were back together again, her daughter would forgive her.

The front door to the cathedral was unlocked, and she slipped quietly inside. Through the dim lighting, she could see Father Andrews sitting in a front pew with his head bent in prayer. As tears gathered in her eyes, she held her daughter close for one last moment, breathing in her smell and relishing the feel of her head against her shoulder.

I can't do this, she thought, her soul in torment.

"Is everything alright?"

With a gasp, she jerked back when a hand lightly touched her elbow, and she opened her eyes to see Father Andrews staring at her with worry is his eyes. *You're doing this for her safety,* she told herself. *You don't have any other choice.*

"I...I can't explain right now," she said as she gently placed her daughter in his arms, "but I need you to look after her. I'll be back as soon as I can, but please promise you'll guard her with your life and won't tell anyone I've left her with you. Please?"

His brow wrinkling, he studied her for a

moment, taking in the fear-filled eyes and sweat beading from her brow. "Sister, if you're in trouble, please let me help…"

"No," she shook her head. Reaching out to clutch his arm in desperation, she said, "Please. You're the only one who can help me."

With a sigh, he nodded his head, and she kissed her daughter one last time. Reaching up to touch the locket around her neck, she took it off, hurriedly pulled the photo from its tiny encasement, and scratched a note on the back. After replacing the photo, she pressed the locket into Father Andrews' hand and, motioning to the stuffed, golden-brown bear her daughter held, she said, "I know this is all very strange, but please…sew this locket into the back of her bear, and keep…keep telling her that I love her."

With a muted sob, she turned and ran from the church, the sound of her daughter screaming out for her shattering her heart into a million pieces. The church door slammed shut behind her, and she stumbled off into the night as hot tears poured down her cheeks. *I'll see her again,* she told herself. *I'll be back in a few days, and we'll leave this place for good.*

Spotting her car just up ahead, she quickened her pace and pulled the keys from her purse. Maybe she was going to make it. Maybe...

She reached out to grab the door handle when, suddenly, a figure leaped from the shadows and struck her on the back of the head. Stars floated before her eyes as she sank to the ground, and just before everything went black, a tear trickled down her cheek because she knew with a sinking heart that she would never see her daughter again.

CHAPTER 1

PRESENT DAY
Cloud Haven, Georgia

A cold breeze whistled down the narrow street as Misty Raven stared at the old white church in disbelief. She wrapped her sweater tightly around herself as she tried to ward off a chill that wasn't only related to the weather, but also to the shocking discovery she'd just made.

"If my mother really was that Spanish teacher, I don't think she just disappeared; I think she was murdered, and I've got to find out why."

The words had just passed her lips, but she could barely wrap her mind around their meaning. For eight long years she'd been searching for answers about her past, and now, suddenly, a piece to the puzzle appeared before her in a place she was least expecting it.

"Misty, what's going on?"

Misty was so caught up in her thoughts that she'd almost forgotten she wasn't alone. Turning, she looked up at Brice Barlow, a friend from her new home in Shady Pines, Georgia. The two had traveled to Cloud Haven to buy some custom-built furniture for the old bed-and-breakfast Misty had recently purchased, and on their way home, they were driving by this little church when Misty suddenly asked Brice to stop.

"A flashback," she said in a hoarse whisper, her entire body trembling as she turned to face the church once again. "Ever since I was little, I've had this dream," she continued softly. "Everything is dark and someone is carrying me, but I can't see their face; all I can see are streetlights flashing randomly above my head. I...I'm frightened, and I sense that whoever is carrying me is frightened as well. Just before the dream ends, I see something looming up before us in the night, like a giant silhouette against a dark sky, but I've never been able to figure out what it was." Turning back to look at Brice, Misty clutched his arm and said, "It was the steeple of this church, Brice. This is the place I've been looking for."

Eight years ago, right after her twentieth birthday, Misty discovered a locket sewn into the stuffed folds of her only childhood possession: a teddy bear she'd had for as long as she could remember.

Misty was abandoned when she was three years old and had no memories of her parents. The stuffed toy was the only link to her past, and she was shocked to find that it held a secret. Inside the locket was a tiny, black-and-white photograph of a woman holding a baby. The photo was blurry and the woman's face was almost completely covered by her dark, curly hair, but Misty knew it was her mother. On the back of the photograph were the scribbled words *"Look for me in the sky"*, and it was then that Misty decided to embark on a journey to find answers. She just wasn't expecting to find them here in Cloud Haven.

"Misty, are you sure?" Brice asked, his eyes wide with shock.

Misty nodded. "Yes, I'm positive," she stated. "I've been here before, Brice. I can feel it."

Another chill swept over her body as she slowly looked around, trying to make sense of the jumbled memories and random flashbacks. If she was correct in her assumptions, this was the last place she'd seen her mother. But why had she chosen to leave Misty here? None of it made sense.

"Life doesn't always make sense, but that's no excuse to give up. You've got to keep trying, no matter what."

The words of Misty's beloved Mr. Sikes floated through her mind just then, and she took a deep breath, trying to calm the whirling thoughts in her head. Mr. Sikes was her last foster family's elderly neighbor; he'd taken Misty under his wing and became more like a grandfather to her. He'd always known what to say to make her stop and think things through in a calm, levelheaded manner, and if not for him, she wouldn't be where she was today. After working as a contractor for over thirty years, he taught Misty everything he knew, and then left his house to her when he passed away. When Misty discovered the locket, she sold the house and used the funds to start her journey toward finding answers.

"Do you want to go inside?"

Brice's question interrupted her thoughts and Misty blinked, her heart accelerating a little at the thought of going into the church. Would she be faced with more flashbacks, or would she simply not recognize anything? Either option made her feel tense and anxious, and she took another deep breath before slowly nodding her head in agreement.

As the two quietly walked toward the old structure that stood so proud with its tall, white steeple and circular stained-glass window above the front entranceway, Misty felt an odd combination of both peace and foreboding. Why couldn't she clearly remember what happened that night? Why were her memories so dark and jumbled?

When they reached the front door, Misty held her breath and waited as Brice turned the handle. The church appeared to have been built in the early 1800s, and a sign out front proudly declared it to be "The First Baptist Church of Cloud Haven".

With a creak, the door opened and they stepped quietly into the dimly lit vestibule. The interior of the church hadn't been updated in at least thirty years, but the old woodwork and mahogany pews that lined the sanctuary just ahead were exquisite and obviously well taken care of.

Misty stood very still and silent for a moment,

taking it all in. No clear memories of ever being here before jumped out at her, but something about this place felt so familiar. The smell of old wood, the way the light filtered in through the stained-glass window, and the unique altar which consisted of a depiction of Jesus healing the sick with two angels on either side…it was like Déjà vu. Misty knew she'd been here before; she simply couldn't pin down the memories that floated just beyond her reach.

"Can I help you?" a voice to their right spoke out, and they both turned to find a man in his fifties poking his head from what appeared to be a small office.

"I hope so," Brice replied with a friendly smile. After introducing the two of them, he said, "We're hoping to find some information about something that took place here in this church twenty-five years ago."

"Well, it just so happens that I began pastoring the church around that time," the man said as he stepped toward them to shake their hands. "My name is Jonas Alvin."

At the mention of his taking over the church around the time of her abandonment, Misty felt her heart kick into overdrive. Was this the man with whom she'd been left that night? Could he possibly have the answers she'd been seeking her whole life?

Uncertain of how to address a man of the cloth, Misty cleared her throat and said, "Mr. Alvin, I believe my mother left me here twenty-five years ago. I don't know the details or circumstances, as I was only three at the time, but a man of the cloth took me to a police station in Atlanta where I was then placed in the foster system. Do...do you know anything about that?"

His brow furrowing, Pastor Alvin shook his head and said, "No, I'm very sorry to say I don't."

Misty felt her heart sink and, as if sensing her frustration, Brice gave her hand a squeeze.

"Wouldn't the foster system have that information, though?" Pastor Alvin asked.

"My records, along with hundreds of others, were lost in a fire when I was seven," she replied softly, her tone filled with defeat.

"Perhaps you have the wrong town?" he asked, tilting his head as he studied her. "I've never heard of anyone leaving their child here, and in such a small town as this, I'm sure I would have."

"Maybe you're right," Misty said, finally allowing a small, disheartened sigh to pass her lips. Forcing a smile, she added, "Thank you for your time."

As they turned to go, Misty felt lower than she had in months. She'd thought that after eight years of searching, she'd finally found the right place. How had she gotten it so wrong? Was she so desperate to find the truth that she'd only seen what she wanted to see?

Sensing her dampened spirits, Brice patted Misty on the shoulder and said in a low tone,

"Don't worry; we'll keep looking."

They'd just made it back to the truck when Misty heard the church door open and Pastor Alvin call out to them.

"You know," he said as he walked toward them, "I was just thinking that the church was going through quite a lot during the time period you mentioned. With the decline in attendance, the Catholic church decided to sell, and that's when our congregation bought the place and moved in. The priest, Father Andrews, was in charge at the time all of this was taking place, and he moved to Savannah shortly after. Perhaps he would know something about your situation, Miss Raven."

Once again, Misty felt her hopes rise. "Do you happen to know where he lives?" she asked.

After writing the address to a retirement community where Father Andrews lived, along with a small note, Pastor Alvin touched Misty's arm and said in a kind, sincere voice, "I hope you find what you're looking for."

"I hope so, too," she replied with a smile.

Her eyes alight with hope once again, Misty was about to ask Brice if he'd go to Savannah with her when she suddenly realized the sky had been overtaken with angry, black clouds while they were inside the church.

"I was going to suggest we pay Father Andrews a visit now, but it looks like we're in for some bad weather," Misty said as she and Brice climbed into his truck.

Glancing through the windshield at the sky, he nodded. "Yeah, the weather channel said it's supposed to get pretty bad this evening. Maybe we can go to Savannah sometime next week?"

"Okay," Misty replied, although she knew he wouldn't be able to go until the following Saturday when he was off work.

I'll just go by myself, she thought, unable to stand the thought of waiting a whole week.

As they drove, Misty thought over all the information she'd gathered since her recent move to Shady Pines. Twenty-five years ago, three high-school girls went missing over the course of a year. They all left behind a goodbye note but had yet to return or even try to contact their parents. A couple of weeks ago, Misty talked to Patrick Donovan, a retired schoolteacher, and he said the police investigated the situation and the parents even hired a private detective, but no information on the girls' whereabouts was ever uncovered. Misty also discovered that the girls' Spanish teacher, Elena, disappeared during that time as well, but no one seemed to remember her last name. Misty suspected that Elena was her mother, but she couldn't be entirely certain of anything just yet.

"Brice, I can't help but think that my mother, if she really *was* my mother, and the disappearance of those girls is connected," she stated after several moments of silence. "I know it was never proven that they were killed or kidnapped, and they all supposedly left behind a goodbye note, but everyone I've talked to seems to think there's more to it than that, and I tend to agree. How can I find out more? Do you know any of the parents?"

Brice nodded, and a lock of blonde hair fell across his forehead. "Jessica Hendricks' parents attend my church…well, Mrs. Hendricks attends, while Mr. Hendricks just tags along with her," he added with a chuckle, "and they're constantly updating their mansion of a house, so they come into the store often to pick out new paint colors and such. Why don't you come to church with us on Sunday? I can introduce you to both of them then."

Misty blinked. She'd never been to a church service a day in her life, and the thought of going now made her feel a bit nervous. It would, however, be a great place to meet new people, and Misty was surprised she hadn't already thought of it.

"Sure, that would be great," she agreed. "Thank you so much for everything, Brice."

"You know I'm always happy to help, Misty," Brice said warmly as he glanced over at her. "Church starts at eleven o'clock, by the way; I'll save you a seat."

They continued to talk about the case and had just arrived in town when Brice said, "You know, Misty, Tabitha's parents just opened an antique store on Main Street."

Misty's eyes widened with excitement. "Do you think we have time to stop in before the storm hits?"

Brice nodded and turned his truck down Main Street.

"You'd better go in by yourself," he said after parking in front of a large brick building. "Mrs. O'Reilly will talk my ears off if I go in, and you won't have a chance to ask questions."

The bell above the door jingled as Misty entered the small, newly renovated store, and she smiled politely as a tall, slender woman in her early sixties walked her way.

"Hello, and welcome to O'Reilly's Antiques," the woman said, her blue-green eyes sparkling. "I'm Catherine O'Reilly."

"Hello, Mrs. O'Reilly. I'm Misty Raven," Misty replied as she shook the woman's hand.

"It's so nice to meet you, Misty. Please, call me Catherine. You're the one who recently bought the old…"

"Bed and breakfast," Misty finished the sentence for her with a chuckle. "Yes, ma'am. It seems that everyone in town knows who I am."

"That's part of the joy…or aggravation…of living in a small town," Catherine said with a tinkling laugh. Turning to wave her hand around the showroom, she asked, "Is there something I can help you find?"

I hope so.

"I, uh, was wondering if you have any kitchen items?" Misty stammered, suddenly realizing she needed to buy something if she wanted to get any information out of Mrs. O'Reilly. Luckily, she hadn't decorated her kitchen just yet, and a few antiques to sit around would be perfect. "My kitchen renovations are finished, and I'd love to find a few antiques to decorate with."

Her eyes lighting up, Catherine said, "Oh, yes, I have some mason jars, an old scale, a couple of rolling pins, and the cutest toaster you've ever seen."

After choosing what she wanted from the variety of antiques Catherine showed her, they both carried the items to the front counter and chatted about the town and weather while Catherine scanned each item. Once she was finished and began placing them into bags, Misty cleared her throat and said casually, "Catherine, if it wouldn't be too presumptuous of me to ask, do you remember your daughter's Spanish teacher?"

All the color left Catherine's face as she stopped what she was doing and looked up at Misty.

"My…my daughter?"

Misty nodded, feeling a little hesitant at the ashen look on Catherine's face at the mere mention of her daughter. "Yes," she replied, smiling gently. "Her name is Tabitha, isn't it?"

"That's right," Catherine said, her voice cracking slightly. "No one hardly talks of her anymore. I haven't s-seen her in so long."

"I'm sorry," Misty said, her heart clenching. "If you'd rather not talk about her…"

"No, it's alright," Catherine interrupted, her lower lip trembling. "Just because we rarely speak of her doesn't mean I don't think about her every day. I've wondered so many times if she's…" she stopped and shook her head. "No, I refuse to think that way. Since we don't know for sure, that means there's still hope, right?"

"Yes, that's right," Misty said, reaching out to pat Catherine's hand.

Pulling a tissue from a nearby box, Catherine wiped her eyes and asked, "What…what was your question again, dear?"

Misty took a deep breath and asked once again, "Do you remember Tabitha's Spanish teacher?"

The pause before Catherine answered seemed to last an eternity. "Mrs. Himmel?" she finally said. "Yes, I remember her."

CHAPTER 2

Misty could hardly believe her ears. Finally, someone who remembered her mother's last name!

"Did Mrs. Himmel have any children?" Misty finally asked, attempting to keep her tone neutral and nonchalant as Catherine finished wrapping up Misty's purchases.

Shrugging, Catherine said, "I wouldn't know. I only saw her a couple of times at the school; **she** and her husband seemed very private and mostly kept to themselves."

Tamping down the moan of frustration that threatened to escape the back of her throat, Misty forced a smile and said, "Well, thank you very much for helping me find these wonderful items for my kitchen. It was nice to meet you, Catherine."

As Misty turned to leave, Catherine spoke out, "If you don't mind my asking, dear, why did you ask about Tabitha and Mrs. Himmel?"

Misty hesitated as she tried to decide how much to reveal. *You've got to be honest with these people if you want the same in return,* she told herself.

Turning back to face Catherine, Misty took a deep breath and told her exactly what she'd told Pastor Alvin, while adding that she also suspected Elena Himmel was her mother. Once she was finished, Catherine's eyes were filled with tears and she said sympathetically, "You poor thing. I hope you find what you're looking for, honey. I'm just sorry I wasn't of more help to you."

"Thank you," Misty said. Hesitating for a quick second, she tilted her head and asked, "Catherine, do you believe that your daughter and the other two girls and even Elena Himmel really left of their own free will?"

Misty hated to be so frank and didn't wish to appear rude or uncaring, but she knew she'd never get any answers if she didn't press the matter.

"I...I don't know," Catherine said in a small voice. Glancing around the shop, as if making certain no one was listening, she added with a sniffle, "I've always wondered if someone took my sweet girl and made it look like she left on her own, but I j-just can't stand to think that someone hurt her or even..."

"I understand," Misty said when Catherine's words fizzled out. "Did Tabitha ever do or say anything to make you think she would run away?"

"No," Catherine stated, shaking her head firmly. "We were always so close; I never would have thought she would do something like that."

Misty thanked Catherine once again and left, and as soon as she stepped from the store, she noticed that the wind had picked up considerably in the last fifteen minutes. Hurrying to Brice's truck, she carefully placed her purchases in the back seat and climbed in.

"How did it go?" Brice immediately asked.

"Well, I spent $53," she replied drolly, smirking.

With a laugh, Brice shook his head as he backed out of the parking space. "Leave it to a woman to always find an excuse to buy something," he said.

"I believe it helped, though," she replied with a mysterious wink.

Brice glanced her way and raised his eyebrows. "Are you going to keep me in the dark or what?"

Leaning closer, Misty clutched his arm, barely able to contain her excitement as she said, "Elena's last name was Himmel."

"That's wonderful!" Brice cried. He started to say something else but paused, his eyes widening as he said, "Misty, I'm pretty sure the name Himmel means "sky" in German. That would explain why your mother wrote *"Look for me in the sky"* on the back of the photograph in your locket."

Misty shook her head in disbelief. "I can hardly believe all of this is finally unfolding; I just can't seem to wrap my mind around it."

"I know," Brice replied. "Did Mrs. O'Reilly tell you anything else?"

"Only that she never would have dreamed her daughter would run away and that there's possibly more to it than that," Misty stated with a sigh. "I'm sticking with my theory, Brice; those girls didn't just run away. Something happened to them."

Brice turned down the long, pine-shaded driveway that led to Misty's house and nodded his head. "I agree, but you probably shouldn't share that with everyone just yet."

"I won't," she promised. Gathering up her purchases as Brice parked in front of her house, she smiled at him and said, "Thanks again for all of your help. See you at church in the morning."

Waving goodbye, she hopped from the truck and hurried up the front porch steps. The wood creaked beneath her feet, and she took note of all the work that needed to be done on the L-shaped wraparound porch. Built in 1886, the old Queen Ann Victorian house was in desperate need of repairs when Misty bought it a few months ago. She'd already made a huge dent in the renovations, but still had quite a ways to go.

The wind whipped and whistled through the pine trees as Misty unlocked the front door and went inside. The house was dark and full of shadows, and she hurriedly flipped on the overhead lights; storms always made her feel uneasy, and being surrounded by light calmed her nerves a bit.

Misty could hear Wally, her rescued St. Bernard mix, barking from the kitchen, and she hurried through the house to let him outside before it started raining.

"Yeah, yeah, I know you missed me," she greeted Wally with a chuckle as he pranced happily around her legs, his tail bouncing back and forth. "I missed you, too, you big lug," she added, bending to press a kiss to the top of his huge, soft head.

She let Wally out the back door to do his business and walked into the yard with him, shivering as she wrapped her arms tightly around her waist. It was rare for South Georgia to get much cold weather, even in December, but with the storm blowing in, the temperature was dropping at a surprising rate.

A rumble of thunder sounded in the distance, and Misty called for Wally to come inside. After taking a quick shower, she had just gone back into the kitchen to fix herself a bite to eat when the rain started. Glancing out the kitchen window, Misty's eyes widened at the heavy sheets of rain that blew sideways from the force of the wind. Pine straw and pine cones fell rapidly from the treetops, and when a few of the cones loudly began to strike the top of the roof, Misty hoped none of the limbs would break off and hit the house.

Wally stuck by Misty's side as she chopped some chicken and vegetables for a stir fry. She patted his head reassuringly, wondering if he was frightened of the storm or trying to protect her from the sound of the howling wind and pounding rain coming from outside. Once the food was ready, Misty sat down to eat, her mind filled with thoughts of the day. She was thrilled to have finally found the place she'd been searching for the last eight years, but she was also a bit worried about what she might uncover. What if the truth was too painful to bear?

"I know it was never proven that those girls were killed or kidnapped...but everyone I've talked to thinks there's more to it than that."

Misty's conversation with Brice suddenly drifted through her mind, and she paused with a fork full of food halfway to her mouth. A thought was niggling in the back of her mind, and she sat her fork down to hurry through the house and into her bedroom, with Wally pattering along at her side. Opening her large walk-in closet, she sat on the floor and pulled a box from underneath her clothes. The box was filled with notes and newspaper clippings she'd collected over the last eight years, and she took them out to slowly look over each of them.

Moments ticked by, and the storm continued to rage outside with bouts of thunder randomly rattling the house, but Misty didn't budge from her seated position on the closet floor as she pored over the contents of the box in disbelief. She'd collected so much information in the last eight years; why hadn't she noticed this before?

She was so focused on the clippings that when Wally nudged her shoulder and licked her on the cheek, she jerked in surprise. Raising wide eyes to stare at her furry companion, she whispered, "Wally, this has to be more than a coincidence. Right?"

Misty paper-clipped the articles that were the most similar together and placed them in the small safe she kept in the back of her closet. Her mind was so jumbled that she could barely focus as she got ready for bed, and after attempting to read for almost an hour, she finally gave up and turned out the lights. She didn't expect to fall asleep so quickly, but the tiring day had apparently taken its toll; she was asleep within minutes.

Muffled voices began trickling into the deep recesses of Misty's mind, but she couldn't quite make out the words being spoken. It sounded like an argument, and then a loud crash suddenly echoed throughout the house just as the pounding of footsteps reached Misty's ears. Her heart accelerated as she began to feel tense and afraid, and she pressed herself back against the bed in an attempt to hide.

Suddenly, two figures appeared within a contorted doorway just across the room. Misty couldn't see their faces, but they seemed to be struggling, and she felt hot tears spilling down her cheeks as she watched what appeared to be a fight to the death.

Just then, there was a loud *thump*, and Misty heard a deep, guttural groan as one figure slumped slowly to the floor.

"It's okay, sweetheart," a trembling voice said.

Just then, a low growl sounded near Misty's ear, and she spun to see a dark figure lurking near her bathroom door. She gasped as it came charging toward her, hands outstretched, and she tried to scream, but no sound would come out. She lay there, frozen in place, as it drew closer and closer and closer…

Her eyes popping open, Misty sat up in bed and shoved herself back against the headboard, her shoulder blades striking the wood with a sharp *crack*. Hardly noticing the pain, Misty's entire body shook as she frantically searched the pitch-black room, and with trembling fingers, she reached out to fumble for the lamp.

With a *click,* the bedroom was bathed in light, and Misty saw Wally sitting by her side, watching her intently. He stood up and nudged her leg with his nose, his eyes searching hers as if to ask if she was okay.

"I…I'm alright, buddy," she said, her voice breathless and weak.

Taking a deep breath, Misty pushed herself out of bed and walked slowly into the bathroom to wash her sweat-drenched face and neck. She'd had dreams her entire life, which she'd realized when she was a teenager were more like flashbacks from her past, but they'd always been the same; she'd never had one like this before, and it left her feeling drained and frightened.

After washing her face and changing her pajamas, Misty went back to bed but left the lamp on this time. She lay there for almost an hour, wondering what this dream had meant and who the two people were she'd witnessed struggling. Was the woman who spoke her mother? If so, who was the other person, and why had it seemed like murder was their intent?

CHAPTER 3

Misty barely slept for the rest of the night and finally got up just before six o'clock. With bleary eyes and mussed hair, she slipped into her robe and left Wally sleeping in his bed as she tiptoed quietly through the dark house and into the kitchen to fix herself some coffee. She listened as the wind blew gently through the pine trees out back, shivering as she stood in the quiet, cold kitchen and filled the coffee maker with fresh, aromatic grounds. While the coffee percolated, she rubbed her bare arms and puttered back into the living room to turn up the heat. The house creaked and moaned in its old age, something that Misty had finally grown used to, but with the shadows in the room and the way the wind whispered outside, she suddenly felt a sense of wariness creep over her.

That nightmare just has you on edge, she told herself. Walking across the den, she'd just nudged the thermostat upward when she thought she heard footsteps on her front porch. Her brow furrowing, she flipped off the lamp by the sofa and slid through the pitch-dark living room toward the foyer, her ears listening intently for any more sound.

When Misty reached the cold, dark foyer, she stood completely still and silent, her eyes glued to the front door. Had her disturbing dream and sleepless night left her nerves on edge, or was someone really out there? And if so, who could it possibly be so early in the morning?

It's probably another raccoon, she thought, remembering the night a rather large and bold raccoon had scratched frantically at the back door during a storm and nearly scared her half to death.

When no other sound met her ears, Misty shook her head and turned to go back to the kitchen, only to stop dead in her tracks when a very audible creak sounded just on the other side of the front door. Her heart in her throat, Misty reached out and flipped on the front porch light, gasping in fright when the large shadow of a man loomed from the other side of the privacy glass.

"Who...who's there?" she called out, her voice shaking.

The shadow moved then, as if looking directly at her, and suddenly Misty heard Wally begin to bark ferociously from her bedroom. The hair stood up on the back of her neck, and Misty glanced around frantically for a weapon.

"Miss Raven?" an unfamiliar voice called out, giving her pause.

"Y-yes?" she responded, heart in her throat.

"I'm sorry to just show up like this, but my name is Luxton O'Reilly and I'd like to speak with you for a moment."

Misty blinked in surprise, wondering why on earth a man she'd never met before would show up on her doorstep, uninvited, and an hour before sunrise.

"Just a moment," she said, hurrying into her bedroom to get Wally. He bounded past her and into the foyer, his tail down and ears back, and she had to hurry to catch up to him. Grabbing the leash that hung by the front door, Misty hooked it to his collar and told him to "be quiet". He immediately stopped barking, but kept his eyes trained on Misty as she cautiously unlocked and opened the front door.

"How can I help you, Mr. O'Reilly?" she asked, peering cautiously through the crack in the door at the large, muscular man before her.

Noting the leash in her hand, Mr. O'Reilly cleared his throat and said, "I know we've never met, but my wife told me of your visit to our antique store yesterday and the questions you asked about our daughter."

Raising her eyebrows, Misty asked, "Yes?"

Luxton O'Reilly ran his fingers through his short, white-gray hair, his jaw clenching. He was a large man, with a white goatee, firm jawline, and tan, leathered skin. To say that he looked foreboding was an understatement, and Misty wondered why such a pretty, classy lady such as Catherine had ever married him. When he turned his cool, blue eyes to stare directly into hers, Misty immediately felt herself go on guard at the look on his face

"I would appreciate it if you stayed away from my wife from now on," he said, his voice low. "Catherine gets very upset when the subject of our daughter is broached, and your nosy questions are out of line. Our daughter is not your business, Miss Raven."

Wally let out a low growl at the tension he felt between Misty and Luxton, and she tightened her hold on his leash.

"Mr. O'Reilly, I'm only trying to find answers about my past," she told him, "and I believe those answers may involve the disappearance of your daughter. Don't you want to find the truth of what happened, too?"

"My daughter ran away," he snapped. "She left a note, and there was a thorough investigation afterward. Nothing was ever found, and my wife was completely heartbroken; she has never been the same since." Taking a step closer to Misty, he added in a warning tone, "You'll do yourself a favor if you do as I say, Miss Raven, and keep your nosy questions to yourself."

He spun on his heel then and stomped away, leaving Misty to stare after him open-mouthed. It wasn't until later that she realized he'd said only his *wife's* heart was broken after their daughter's disappearance, and not both of their hearts.

Five hours later, Misty made certain to arrive at church a few minutes early. The day had barely even started, and she already felt exhausted. As she stepped inside and looked around for the Barlow family, she smoothed down her A-line hunter green dress and flipped her long, curly black hair over her shoulder. She spotted Catherine O'Reilly and a few other people she recognized, and she stopped to speak to those nearest to her.

"Misty, you look great," a familiar voice spoke from behind, and Misty turned to find Tori Barlow, Brice's cousin, walking inside with an off-white coat folded over one arm. She and Tori had become instant friends when they first met, and since Tori volunteered at the animal shelter, she was the one responsible for bringing Wally and Misty together.

"Thanks," Misty replied, smiling at her lovely friend. Tori wore a sapphire blue turtleneck sweater that beautifully accentuated her blue eyes, and her strawberry blonde hair was swept up into a graceful French twist. "So do you."

"Come on," Tori said, grabbing her friend by the hand as she nodded toward the sanctuary. "Brice and my family are saving us seats."

The church was quite large and beautifully decorated for Christmas, with poinsettias, red bows, and garland placed tastefully about. Tori stopped to introduce Misty to a few people along the way, and by the time they made it to their seats, the music was just beginning. Misty smiled at Brice as she slid in to the pew beside him, not failing to notice how handsome he looked in his gray plaid sports coat. Mrs. Amy, Tori's mother, leaned around to smile at Misty, while her husband, Mr. Neil, gave a friendly nod and wave.

For the next hour, Misty relaxed and enjoyed her first church service. The music and singing were beautiful, and the message the pastor gave was stirring. Once the service was over, Brice took Misty by the hand and led her across the church to introduce her to a couple in their early sixties. Huey and Darlene Hendricks were Jessica's parents, and Misty was immediately struck by how mismatched the pair seemed. It was apparent that Huey had been quite handsome in his day, and he was very friendly and even a little flirtatious. Darlene, on the other hand, was quiet and more withdrawn, with an ample figure and a tight, stoic expression.

"We heard how you helped solve Cora and Hank's murders," Huey said to Misty, his eyes alight with interest. "You were almost killed yourself, weren't you?"

Misty nodded. "Yes, I was," she replied. After a slight hesitation, she added, "I'm actually attempting to solve another mystery…one that took place around the time of your daughter's disappearance."

Raising his eyebrows in surprise, Huey tilted his head and asked, "What do you mean?"

"This may sound strange, but I believe that Jessica's Spanish teacher, Mrs. Himmel, was my mother. Do you remember her?"

"Elena was your mother?" Huey asked, his eyes widening. "Why, yes, of course I remember her. We actually had lunch together once."

Misty blinked in surprise, but before she could respond, Darlene stepped in and said, "They bumped in to each other at the same restaurant one afternoon and just decided to eat together; it wasn't planned."

Misty saw a look pass between Mr. and Mrs. Hendricks, one that she couldn't quite interpret, but Mrs. Hendricks didn't look very happy and it wasn't hard to feel the tension in the air.

Clearing her throat awkwardly, Misty asked, "Do either of you know whether she had a child?"

"I don't think so," Darlene stated with a sniff.

"I'm fairly certain she did," Huey said at almost the same time. "I think she even mentioned a child when we were having lunch."

"Well, *I* talked to her on more than one occasion about Jessica's grades, and she never said anything about having a daughter of her own," Mrs. Hendricks snapped.

"Well, maybe she didn't find it as easy to talk to you as she did to me," he returned smugly.

Attempting to keep the couple on track before they ended up in a full-fledged argument, Misty handed them her locket and asked, "I know it's hard to tell, but does this look like Elena?"

"It does," Huey replied, nodding as he studied the picture. "Her hair was dark and curly like that, and she was very petite, like the woman in the picture."

"You certainly *do* remember her, don't you?" Darlene muttered, her jaw clenching, and Misty didn't miss the way she self-consciously smoothed her shirt down over her ample hips.

Ignoring his wife's obvious irritation, Huey handed the locket back to Misty with a smile and asked pleasantly, "Is there anything else I can help you with?"

Once again, Misty paused, uncertain of how much she should ask a couple she'd only just met, especially when Mrs. Hendricks obviously disapproved. Before she could decide, however, Brice stepped in.

"Do either of you remember noticing anything odd before Jessica disappeared?" he asked.

"Before she left, you mean?" Huey corrected.

"We don't know that she *left,* Huey," Darlene snapped.

Mr. Hendricks sighed, as if trying to remain patient. "She left a note behind, Darlene," he stated matter-of-factly.

"But don't you remember how she…"

"Look, we've got a chicken in the oven, so we'd best be getting home," Huey interrupted his wife. Smiling tightly at Misty and Brice, he took Darlene's arm and said, "It was nice meeting you, Miss Raven."

As they watched the couple hurry away, Misty commented to Brice, "I wonder what Mrs. Hendricks was about to say."

Brice shrugged. "I don't know, but whatever it was, Mr. Hendricks didn't want her to say it."

Before they could discuss it further, Tori and Mrs. Amy approached Misty and asked her to join them for lunch. Misty readily agreed, and as she walked out with the Barlow's, she was introduced to the pastor and was immediately struck by how kind he seemed.

"I hope we'll see you again next Sunday," Pastor Williams said with a warm smile.

"Yes, sir, I believe you will," Misty replied, shaking his hand.

As Misty headed to her car, she noticed Mr. and Mrs. Hendricks driving away in a very expensive Mercedes-Benz SUV, and it looked as if they were in the middle of a very heated argument.

CHAPTER 4

T he next morning, Misty was preparing breakfast when her cellphone chimed, and she pulled it from the pocket of her robe to read the text message that lit up the screen.

"Good morning. How are you?"

The text was from Adam Dawson, the local electrician who had befriended her while doing some work in her house. They had gone out a couple of times, but Misty hadn't heard from him since Thanksgiving.

"Good, and you?"

"I'm good," he replied. *"Been working up in the mountains of North Georgia since the day after Thanksgiving and have had no cellphone reception. I just got back last night. Want to grab some lunch?"*

Misty agreed and, after quickly eating a bowl of oatmeal, got to work on the house for a few hours before her date with Adam.

It's not a date, she told herself later, as she got ready. She'd never dated much, and although Adam was a very nice guy, she wasn't ready to settle down with anyone just yet. She still had too much to uncover about her past and didn't want to get distracted. She had to admit to herself, though, that Adam was very nice…and not too hard on the eyes, either.

Adam arrived at five minutes to twelve, and Misty greeted him at the front door with a smile. He wore a pair of dark brown corduroy pants, a beige shirt, and a matching beige sweater, which nicely accentuated his black hair and olive complexion.

They drove into town and parked in front of *Pat's Kitchen,* a cozy little café that served a variety of homemade soups, salads, and sandwiches. The restaurant was previously owned by Daniel Abraham, but after his death a few weeks prior, Patrick Donovan purchased the place and had just re-opened a few days ago.

"I haven't been here yet, have you?" Adam asked as they stepped inside the restaurant.

Misty shook her head but didn't respond; all she could think of was the last time she was in this room and how traumatic of a night that was.

"Hello, you two," a voice spoke out from their left, and Misty turned to see Mr. Owens sitting at the nearest table.

"Hi, Mr. Owens, how are you?" she asked with a friendly smile.

Misty first met Mr. Owens, owner of Owens Security, about a month ago when he came to her house to install her security system. He was eating alone, and Misty couldn't help but notice that the wedding ring he'd been wearing before was now missing. He had bags under his eyes, his uniform shirt was wrinkled, and his gray hair was mussed from wearing a baseball cap.

"I'm doing okay, thank you," he replied, returning Adam's nod. "Make sure you try the seafood chowder; it's delicious."

"Adam, Miss Raven, how nice to see you both!"

Before Misty could respond to Mr. Owens, Patrick Donovan appeared from the kitchen and quickly walked across the room to greet them. As always, he looked neat as a pin, and his deep blue eyes were alight with pleasure.

"It's nice to see you, too," she replied, accepting his outstretched hand. "I'm very excited to try your seafood chowder," she added, smiling at Mr. Owens. "I hear it's excellent."

With a broad smile, Patrick said, "I certainly hope you'll think so after you try it. You know, I never would have thought I would go into the restaurant business after retiring from the public school system, but I quickly found that retirement can be pretty boring, especially when you don't have a family to keep you occupied."

"A man needs to keep busy, doesn't he, Mr. Donovan?" Adam asked, clapping Patrick on the back.

They chatted a bit longer before Adam and Misty took their seats, and as they looked over the menu, Misty thought of the conversation she'd had with Patrick a few weeks ago and how curious he'd seemed. She hadn't told him anything, but now that she was being more open with everyone about her past, perhaps she should speak with him again about Elena.

Suddenly, Misty realized she hadn't told Adam anything about her real reasons for coming to Shady Pines, and she needed to do so before someone else did. The only thing she'd ever told him of her past was that she was raised in the foster system; how would he react when he discovered she hadn't been completely honest with him?

"You seem a bit preoccupied," Adam pointed out after they'd placed their orders. "Is something wrong?"

Misty blinked, a bit surprised he could read her so well. Clearing her throat nervously, she sighed and said, "Actually, there *is* something that's bothering me." She stopped and fiddled with her napkin for a moment, trying to figure out what she wanted to say. "We…we've talked a bit about my past, but there are a few things I haven't told you; like the real reason I came to Shady Pines."

As Misty relayed her story, she watched as Adam's expression went from surprise, to interest, to shock, and finally, excitement.

"Misty, you now know your mother's real name," he said, reaching across the table to grasp her hand. "That is wonderful!"

"I agree," she replied with a smile. "So…you're not upset that I haven't already told you all of this?"

Adam shook his head. "No, not at all. I suspected

there was more to your story and knew you'd tell me when you were ready."

The server brought their dessert then, and Misty sat back in her chair with a feeling of relief that he'd taken the news so well. He'd quickly become a very dear friend to her, and she didn't want to lose him.

"When do you plan to go to Savannah to see Father Andrews?" Adam asked after the server left and they began eating the delicious cherry turnover.

"Sometime this week," she replied.

"How about right now?" he asked, his eyes twinkling.

"You want to go with me?" she asked, a bit surprised.

"I never pass up an opportunity to go to Savannah," he replied. Pulling his wallet from his pocket, he paid the bill and stood up, extending his hand out to Misty. "Ready?"

Smiling with excitement, Misty nodded and took his hand. "Definitely."

As they left, Misty told Patrick Donovan that the food was delicious, and she made a mental note to stop back by sometime soon to talk with him about Elena.

It was nearly two o'clock by the time they arrived in one of Misty's favorite cities, and as they followed the GPS to the small retirement community where Father Andrews lived, Misty gazed happily from the car window. The city was decorated for Christmas and even more charming than usual, with striking red poinsettias dotting the sidewalks beneath towering, moss-laden oaks, and red ribbons were tied to the cast iron light poles and fences. Misty had spent a few months in Savannah about three years ago, and her love for this charming city hadn't faded a bit.

"Here it is," Adam muttered, and Misty sat up straighter in her seat to look around.

"This looks like a nice place," she stated as they parked and walked toward the main office. Just beyond the gate, she could see a row of apartment buildings surrounding a charming little pond with picnic tables and a path for walking or biking. Several seniors were out mingling in the sun, some were wearing exercise outfits, and others sat on benches reading books. It looked like a peaceful place, and although Misty had never even met Father Andrews, she was oddly happy to know he lived in such a nice community.

"Can I help you?" the lady at the desk asked when they walked into the front office.

"We're here to see Father Andrews," Misty told her, smiling politely as she handed her the note Pastor Alvin had written along with the address.

"Let me see if he's available," the woman said. "He's often out at the city mission during the early afternoon, but he may still be here."

Misty held her breath as the lady called Father Andrews' apartment and sighed with relief when he finally answered.

After speaking with him for a moment, the lady hung up and told them, "He said he'd love to see anyone that's come from Cloud Haven; I'll open the gate for you."

"Why am I so nervous?" Misty whispered moments later as they hurried up the stairs to Father Andrews' apartment.

"Because for eight years you've been searching for the answers that you may be about to find right now," Adam replied with a chuckle. Reaching out to squeeze her arm, he added, "Don't worry; I'm sure everything will go great."

They'd just found the right apartment number and were about to knock when the door swung open and an elderly gentleman dressed in a black shirt and black pants stepped out.

"I just received a call that Johnny, one of the homeless men at the shelter, has had a bad spell and is asking for me," he said, his voice deep and raspy. Patting them both on the shoulder, he added, "Why don't you two walk to the parking lot with me and tell me why you've come? I don't believe I've ever met you before."

"No, sir, you haven't," Misty said as she and Adam hurried to catch up with the sprightly old gentleman. She quickly introduced Adam and herself, and with a deep breath, said, "Father Andrews, I was raised in the foster system and have been trying to track down my family for the last eight years. All I know is that twenty-five years ago, I was left at a church that I believe to be the one in Cloud Haven."

At Misty's words, Father Andrews stumbled and might have possibly fallen if Adam hadn't been quick enough to catch him by the arm. His face had gone pale, and he stopped walking to stare at Misty.

"Are you alright?" Adam asked him.

"Go on," Father Andrews said to Misty, ignoring Adam's question.

"Well," Misty cleared her throat, "I was only three when all of this happened and can't remember much, but a man of the cloth took me to a police station in Atlanta. My records were lost a few years after that, and so the trail ends there. I was hoping you could help me."

As Misty spoke, she couldn't help but notice how wary Father Andrews' expression had become. His eyes began to dart back and forth, as if searching for a quick escape route, and he hurriedly pulled his arm away from Adam.

When he didn't respond, Misty asked hesitantly, "Do you know anything about this, Father Andrews?"

Taking a step back, he shook his head and said in a sharp tone, "I don't care to discuss anything that happened back then. Now, if you'll excuse me, I am needed at the shelter."

Misty stood and watched, open-mouthed, as the

elderly gentleman turned and hurried away without another word.

CHAPTER 5

I can't believe this," Misty breathed, her tone filled with frustration. Turning to look up at Adam, she asked, "Is it just me, or does that man know something but refuses to say what?"

"He definitely knows something," Adam replied as he watched Father Andrews get into his car and drive away. Shaking his head, he looked back at Misty and, with a furrowed brow, asked, "Why would he not want to tell you, though? It doesn't make sense."

"No, it doesn't," she stated, fully annoyed at how the entire day had progressed. With a huff, she spun on her heel and marched back up the stairs.

"Misty, where are you going?" Adam wanted to know as he quickly followed.

Pulling an old receipt from her purse, Misty jotted her name and number on the back and stopped before Father Andrews' door as she folded the piece of paper in half.

"I'm leaving my information in case he decides to change his mind," she replied as she bent to shove the paper under his door. "Maybe once he thinks about it, he'll change his mind and call me."

"You don't give up, do you?" Adam asked with

a chuckle.

"I can't," she stated simply. "I have to know where I came from and what happened to my parents."

His eyes gleaming with admiration, Adam took Misty's hand and said warmly, "I believe you will, Misty."

Smiling, she shrugged and said, "I hope so."

As they headed back to Adam's truck, he asked, "What now?"

"Let's grab a sweet tea and take a walk through Forsyth Park," Misty replied as she buckled her seatbelt. "I need to relax a bit before we head home."

Twenty minutes later, they were strolling silently through the park, a large sweet tea in Misty's hand and a coffee in Adam's. The air was crisp, and the combination of the gentle spray of water from the fountain and soft Christmas music played by a local saxophonist calmed Misty's tangled spirit. She'd come to the park as often as possible when she was staying in Savannah, and she'd missed the gentle beauty and peaceful setting a great deal.

"I don't know why I've never asked this before," Misty suddenly said, breaking the silence, "but do you have any siblings?"

Adam nodded. "I sure do. A younger brother and baby sister."

"That's nice," she said. "I always wanted siblings." After a brief pause, she laughed and added, "I have to admit, though, that I feel a little sorry for your sister."

Raising his eyebrows in surprise, Adam looked at her and asked, "Why is that?"

"I can just imagine how it must have been for her to have two older brothers," Misty replied, smiling. "She was probably teased mercilessly, hardly ever given any privacy, and had to fight for everything she wanted. Am I right?"

"Hey, we taught her some very valuable life lessons at a young age," he stated, lips twitching. "She learned to be tough and not so sensitive about everything, how to bait a fish hook, and that boys have absolutely no sense when they're teenagers."

Misty laughed again. "You're definitely right about the last one. Do she and your brother still live in Shady Pines?"

"Archer joined the army right after high school and is currently stationed in Texas, and Lexi is living in Atlanta; she's a nurse."

"I'm guessing her name is Alexis?" When Adam nodded, Misty smiled and said, "All "a" names; I like that. Do you miss them?"

"Very much," Adam nodded as he threw his empty coffee cup into a nearby trash can. "My brother and I have always been very close, and my sister is the best. She's been a nurse for as long as I can remember; she'd tend to our many scrapes and cuts when we were kids, and make sure we drank enough fluids when we were sick."

"Your mom didn't do those things?" Misty

asked, tilting her head to look up at him.

"Mom always had a weak stomach when it came to blood," Adam replied with a chuckle. "Plus, she worked part time at the bank and wasn't always home."

As Adam continued to talk about his family, Misty felt a twinge of sadness as she thought of her own childhood. She'd never had the stability or guidance provided by parents who love their children and teach them how to be confident and secure adults. Instead, she'd had to learn how to lean on herself and trust in her own abilities, and if not for Mr. Sikes, she wasn't sure where she would have ended up in life. She missed him very much; he was the closest thing she'd ever had to family, and she was grateful for everything he'd taught her.

"Were you very close to any of your foster siblings?"

Adam's question took Misty by surprise, and she slowly nodded her head as she took another sip of her sweet tea.

"Yes," she finally replied softly, her tone somber as she revisited the past. "There was a girl named Gabby who was the same age as me. We were placed with my third foster family at the same time, and we hit it off immediately. I remember feeling so happy that I finally had a sister. I was with that family for almost a year when they had to move to a smaller house; one of their three foster kids had to go, and since I was sickly, they chose me. I was devastated."

The memories of that awful day hadn't haunted Misty in a long time, but she could still feel the heartbreak of having to tell her best friend, her only friend, goodbye. She'd never been quite the same after that, until she met Mr. Sikes, and even he couldn't take the place of someone who'd been like a sister to her.

"Misty, I am so sorry," Adam said, his tone filled with sympathy. "Did you ever see Gabby again?"

Misty shook her head. "No, and I never allowed myself to get close to anymore of my foster siblings after that. It was just too hard."

They continued walking, the silence between them heavy, and Misty struggled to force away the tears that burned the back of her eyes. She hadn't thought of Gabby in years; the memory of losing that family and the abandonment she'd felt afterward was too painful to recall. Now that Adam had broached the subject, however, it all came flooding back, and she suddenly felt an overwhelming urge to cry.

Without saying a word, Adam reached through the space that separated them and took her hand, gently lacing his fingers through hers. Pulling her closer to his side, he said softly, "You're an amazing woman, Misty Raven. With all you've been through, you still manage to keep a smile on that beautiful face of yours." Looking down at her with a smile of his own, he squeezed her hand and added, "You're a very special woman, and I admire you a great deal."

Rarely had anyone said anything so kind to her, and Misty struggled with what to say in return. Glancing down at the walkway beneath their feet, she finally said in a hoarse voice, "Thank you, Adam. That really means a lot."

They continued walking, hand in hand, and the silence between them this time wasn't quite so loud. In fact, it was rather peaceful and serene, like the beautiful fountain that gently sprinkled water into the pool below.

When Adam dropped Misty off at her house later, she thanked him once again for all of his help. As she watched him drive away with a cloud of dust trailing behind his truck, she suddenly felt very grateful for having met him.

As she let Wally outside to do his business, she was unable to resist his big, soulful eyes when he came back moments later with a tennis ball in his mouth. With a smile, she playfully wrestled the ball from him and threw it across the yard. After a few games of fetch, she threw the ball once more and then quickly darted around the side of the house to hide behind some bushes while making a quick whistling sound with her lips. This little game of hide-and-seek had become one of their favorite games. When Wally heard the whistle, he knew that was his cue to find Misty and never failed to do so.

Later that evening, after Misty had eaten supper and taken a shower, she and Wally settled in for the night. As she lay in bed and tried to relax and read a book, she found that she was once again too distracted by thoughts of the day. She couldn't seem to figure out why Father Andrews had acted so mysteriously. If he knew something, why wouldn't he tell her?

CHAPTER 6

The following afternoon, Misty was upstairs sanding the walls in one of the guest bedrooms when she heard a car door slam. Stepping over to the window, she spotted Tori walking up to her house carrying a small, white box, and she hurried downstairs to let her friend inside.

"I hope you don't mind my popping by like this," Tori said as soon as Misty opened the front door, "but I closed the coffee shop early today and wanted you to try these scones I made this morning."

"Why did you close early?" Misty asked, following her friend through the house and into the kitchen.

"The toilet overflowed and ran out into the main room," Tori said with a moan as she placed her hand along the side of her face. "I was so embarrassed; thankfully, I only had two customers at the time."

She continued to rattle on while Misty fixed them both a cup of coffee, and then finally stopped when she noticed how tired Misty looked.

"Is everything alright, Misty?" she wanted to know, eyeing her friend closely.

"A lot has happened in the last forty-eight hours," Misty said with a sigh as she got two mugs from the overhead cabinet.

"What do you mean?"

As Misty poured the freshly brewed coffee into the mugs and retrieved a container of sweet cream from the refrigerator, she told Tori about her trip to Savannah.

"I don't understand why Father Andrews wouldn't want to tell you anything," Tori stated, her forehead wrinkling. "Do you suppose he was involved in your mother's disappearance?"

Shrugging, Misty said, "I have no clue, and Saturday night I had another dream, but this one was different from the others. Nothing makes sense, Tori, and it's so frustrating. And then Mr. O'Reilly showed up at my house yesterday morning before dawn and basically threatened me..."

Sitting up straighter, Tori's eyes widened as she grabbed Misty's arm. "He did *what?*"

Misty relayed everything that happened with Luxton O'Reilly, and by the time she was finished, Tori was pacing around the kitchen in a huff.

"What right does that man think he has for showing up at your house uninvited to tell you to leave his wife alone? Misty, I think you should tell the police."

"If I did that, Officer Lewis would simply tell me

once again to quit being nosy," Misty stated, rolling her eyes.

Since moving to Shady Pines, Misty had had her fair share of run-ins with the local law enforcement, namely Officer Lewis. He'd accused her of stirring up trouble, of poking her nose where it didn't belong, and of asking too many pushy questions. She may have helped him solve a murder that happened in her house fifteen years ago, but she doubted he'd appreciate her opening up yet another cold case.

Tori sat back down and sighed. "You're probably right. You know, I never cared very much for Luxton O'Reilly, and now I can see why; I'm just glad Wally was here with you."

"His wife seems so nice," Misty said, shaking her head. "I don't know how she lives with him."

"Maybe he's nicer to her," Tori chuckled as she reached for another scone. "You won't stop trying to find out what happened, will you?"

Misty shook her head. "Certainly not. I'm actually planning to call the high school where Elena worked and see if I can find out anything there."

"Good plan," Tori nodded approvingly. "You should ask to speak with Principal Kirby; he is a really nice man, and he's worked there for years. He was a teacher at the high school first, then he became the assistant principal, and the school loved him so much that they made him the principal a few years after that. If you tell him you think the Spanish teacher may have been your mother and don't mention that she may have been murdered, I'm sure he'll be happy to help you."

Misty thought over her friend's suggestion and nodded her head in agreement. "I'll do it," she said, her tone filled with determination.

Smiling enthusiastically, Tori started to say something else but stopped, her brow furrowing slightly as she asked, "Did you say that Adam went with you to Savannah, and not Brice?"

"That's right," Misty replied with a nod. "Brice couldn't go until this weekend, and I didn't want to wait that long."

"Was it just me, or was he a little distant at lunch on Sunday?" Tori wanted to know.

Trying to hide a smile, Misty took a sip of her coffee, knowing that her friend wanted to know what had happened between them at Cloud Haven. Finally, she said, "He told me about his ex-fiancé; he said that he isn't sure if he'll ever be ready for another relationship."

Blinking, Tori frowned and asked, "Really? Wow, that's been over for years."

"Well, apparently *he's* not over it yet," Misty shrugged.

Tori chewed on her lip for a moment, her expression thoughtful. "You know," she finally said in a soft voice, "when Brice's dad died, it really threw him. They were so close and Brice's heart was just broken into a million pieces. He pulled away from everyone for months, and if not for dad and Pops, I really don't know what would have happened to him. When things ended between him and Cassie a few years later, his mom had just remarried and moved away, and I think he simply decided he couldn't take anymore heartbreak."

"I can't say that I blame him," Misty said with a sigh, her heart clenching sympathetically for her friend. "That's a lot for a person to deal with."

"You could always help him deal with it," Tori replied with a sly wink.

Chuckling, Misty shook her head and said, "Tori, that's something he's going to have to do on his own. Besides, I'm too busy with the renovations of this place and trying to find answers about my past to get involved with anyone right now. Brice is a good friend, and I want to leave it that way."

Pursing her lips in disappointment, Tori nodded. "Okay, fine, but I think you two would be perfect together."

With a small laugh, Misty quickly changed the subject, and pretty soon they were making plans to visit the new trail the city had recently paved around Lake Laurier.

"We could go in the morning," Tori said. "I doubt I will be able to open the shop tomorrow, anyway."

"Sounds good," Misty replied. "I heard there is a bike rental there, too, so we can ride bikes if you want."

"It's a plan," Tori agreed with a smile. Her cellphone chimed just then, and she stated it was the plumber. "He wants me to meet him at the shop," she said as she gathered up her belongings.

They agreed to meet at the lake at eight the next morning, and Misty waved goodbye to her friend as she drove away.

Feeling renewed with vigor and determination, Misty grabbed her cellphone and called the high school. When the secretary said that Principal Kirby had an availability at one o'clock, Misty tried to contain her excitement. She only hoped he would be as friendly as Tori said, and more agreeable than both Father Andrews and Luxton O'Reilly had been.

CHAPTER 7

At one o'clock sharp, Misty arrived at Shady Pines High to see Principal Kirby. As she walked into his large office, she told herself to stay calm and not mention any suspicions of murder or kidnapping.

"It's nice to meet you, Miss Raven," Principal Kirby said with a friendly smile as he shook Misty's hand. He was tall and slim, with salt-and-pepper hair and striking blue eyes. As he ushered her toward the chair that sat before his desk, he added, "I heard all about how you helped catch Cora Griffin's murderer, and I've been eager to meet you."

"It's nice to meet you, too, Principal Kirby," she replied with a smile as she took her seat.

"Oh, please, call me Glenn," he said, circling around his desk to sit down. Leaning forward, he laced his fingers together and asked, "To what do I owe the pleasure of this visit, Miss Raven?"

Suddenly feeling very nervous, Misty took a deep breath and said, "Uh…well, this is going to seem like an odd question, but do you remember the Spanish teacher that taught here about twenty-five years ago? I believe her name was Elena Himmel."

Principal Kirby blinked in surprise as a wave of confusion passed through his blue eyes. "Yes, I remember her," he replied slowly, pausing to clear his throat. "Why…why do you ask?"

Misty shifted in her seat. "Well, it's just possible that she was my mother."

Principal Kirby stared at Misty for a moment in silence, and she couldn't help but wonder what was going through his mind. Finally, he shook his head and said, "I'm sorry, but you just took me by surprise. Why do you think she was your mother?"

"When I was three years old, I was left at a church by a young woman whom I assume was my mother," Misty replied. "I don't have many memories of that period in my life, but I have this." Taking the locket from around her neck, Misty handed it to him and said, "If you'll look inside, you'll see a small black-and-white photograph of a woman and a baby. Can you tell if that's her? Is it Elena?"

Principal Kirby opened the locket and, pulling a pair of glasses from his shirt pocket, he put them on and studied the picture closely.

"It's hard to tell with her hair shadowing her face like that," he replied after a moment, "but it could be her." Handing the locket back to Misty, he asked, "How can I help you with this, Miss Raven?"

After putting the locket back around her neck,

Misty tucked a stray black curl behind one ear and asked in a hopeful tone, "You wouldn't happen to still have any records dating back twenty-five years, would you?"

Principal Kirby hesitated. "Uh, no, I'm afraid we don't," he replied, shaking his head. "We cleaned out our old files several years ago. I'm very sorry."

Misty nodded. "It's okay; I understand." Tilting her head, she looked at Glenn and asked, "Do you remember anything about her? Like where she and her husband lived, if they had any other children, etcetera?"

Leaning back in his chair, Principal Kirby considered the question for a moment. "I don't believe I ever knew where they lived," he said, his tone thoughtful, "and as for her having any other children, I never knew she had *any* children."

Misty fought back a sigh of frustration. Why couldn't she seem to get a clear answer as to whether or not Elena had children? "I see," she said. "Did you know her very well?"

"Not really," he answered quickly, glancing away from Misty as he picked up a pen and fiddled with it. "We had different schedules, and she also kept to herself a lot, so I saw little of her."

Seeing no reason to stay any longer, Misty nodded and said, "Well, I appreciate your time, Glenn. If you think of anything else, would you mind giving me a call?"

Principal Kirby agreed and, after giving him her number, Misty stood to go. As he walked her out, he said, "I'm sorry I wasn't of more help. It's hard for me to remember the events of last month, let alone twenty-five years ago."

"I understand," Misty smiled.

Waving goodbye, she walked from the school with a feeling of frustration. She'd hoped that the meeting with Principal Kirby would be helpful, but she was leaving with as much information as she'd entered with.

As she drove away from the school, Misty thought over the meeting with Glenn Kirby. He was very nice, just as Tori had said, but he'd almost seemed a little uneasy during their conversation about Elena. Why that was, Misty couldn't say. Unless he knew more than he was admitting?

At four o'clock that afternoon, Misty received a phone call from Officer Lewis. She hadn't seen him since his last call to her house a few weeks ago when she was almost killed, and when he asked her to come down to the station, she wondered what he could possibly want to see her about.

After changing her clothes once again, Misty quickly braided her hair and drove to the station. She was summoned back to Officer Lewis's large corner office immediately, and she smiled hesitantly at him as he stood to beckon her inside. In his mid forties, he stood at an average height, was going bald but still maintained a fringe of brown hair, and his eyes were an odd shade of brown with tiny gold flecks.

"Come in, Miss Raven, and have a seat," he said, motioning to the chair before his desk. Misty did as he asked, eyeing him curiously, and he cleared his throat and said, "I've heard that you've been asking a lot of questions lately about the three girls that disappeared twenty-five years ago and their Spanish teacher, Elena Himmel. Someone said you think she was your mother?"

Nodding, she told him the same story she'd told everyone else, although she suspected he already knew; most of the town probably knew by now. Once she'd finished, she sat back quietly in her chair and waited to hear what he had to say.

Leaning his elbows over onto his desk, Officer Lewis eyed Misty for a moment before he said, "Miss Raven, I understand you want to find out more about your past, but when those girls ran away, it devastated their parents. Digging all of that back up and asking questions is very painful for them, and I don't think you need to continue prying."

"Officer Lewis, I don't think those girls ran away," Misty stated. "I think they were either kidnapped or killed."

Closing his eyes for a moment, Officer Lewis rubbed his forehead and sighed. "And why do you think that?" he asked in a slightly exasperated tone.

"Why would three girls disappear within a few months of each other and never return home?" Misty asked, leaning toward him a bit as she expressed her thoughts. "And not only that, but they've never even called or tried to contact their families. Don't you find that odd, Officer Lewis?"

"Yes, I'll admit that it *is* odd," he nodded, "but those cases were thoroughly investigated and there wasn't a single thing that made us think foul play was involved."

"Mrs. O'Reilly said she never would have thought her daughter would run away," Misty stated stubbornly, "and when I talked to Mrs. Hendricks, she was about to relay something she thought was suspicious, but her husband cut her off."

"Look, Miss Raven," Officer Lewis interrupted in a firm tone, glaring at her disapprovingly, "you may have helped us solve one cold case, but that doesn't give you a free pass to continue meddling in police affairs. I've already heard a couple of complaints about the questions you've been asking, and I'd appreciate it if you'd stop."

This wasn't the first time Misty had butted heads with Officer Lewis, and she raised her chin defiantly, refusing to let him intimidate her further.

"If what I'm doing isn't against the law, then I'm afraid I can't make any promises," she told him.

"Harassment *is* breaking the law, Miss Raven," he snapped, his face growing red.

Misty sighed. "I won't harass anyone, Officer

Lewis, but I deserve to know the truth about my past." When he opened his mouth to say more, Misty raised her hand to stop him. "I promise, though, to do my best not to annoy or upset anyone," she added in a more contrite tone, hoping he would be appeased.

Officer Lewis eyed her skeptically for a moment, and then finally sighed heavily and said, "Alright, I can't really do anything right now but warn you. Just make sure you keep your word, Miss Raven, or I'll be forced to take action."

Misty nodded and, after gathering her purse, quickly left the station before he had the chance to grumble at her any further.

Arriving back home once again, Misty spent the rest of the evening sanding down some of the upstairs walls of her house. As she worked, she kept thinking of her conversation with Officer Lewis. Who could have complained to him? Luxton O'Reilly? The Hendricks'? She understood that rehashing the past was painful for the families, but if finding out the truth was at all possible, why wouldn't they want to do whatever it took to do so?

Misty couldn't help wondering if they also suspected their daughters were murdered and didn't want to face the truth. If so, was it possible they knew more than they were letting on? Had they really told the police everything, or were they all holding something back? Misty couldn't say, but she intended to find out.

CHAPTER 8

Misty arrived at Lake Laurier ten minutes to eight the next morning and climbed from her car to survey the beautiful area that rested just outside of town. Shady Pines had finally paved a trail that circled the heavily wooded, thirty-five-acre lake, and as Misty climbed from her car, it struck her how lonely and isolated the area seemed when no one else was around. The air was cold and damp, and a slight fog still lingered on the ground as the sun hid beneath a layer of gray clouds. Grabbing her windbreaker from the trunk of her car, Misty texted Tori to let her friend know she had arrived.

"I'm running late," Tori responded. *"The plumber called again this morning to let me know he's coming by to try and fix the toilet. He should be here any minute."*

"I'll go ahead and rent a bike and be warming up," Misty told her. *"Text me when you're almost here."*

Walking to a small, covered area where the bicycles were kept, Misty grabbed her credit card, paid the rental fee, and chose an aqua blue bike when the machine unlocked them. After placing her phone into her jacket pocket and zipping it shut, she swung her leg over the seat and headed for the trail.

As she rode, Misty wondered why no one else was around. The area had been a popular fishing and picnicking spot for years, and she'd assumed that the new trail would be a big hit with those looking to enjoy a bit of nature. Perhaps it was going to take some time for everyone to get used to the new spot.

Misty had been riding for nearly ten minutes and was on her second lap around the lake when she felt her phone vibrate in her pocket. Bringing her bike to a stop, she opened her phone to read Tori's text message.

"*On the way,*" she said with a hand-clapping emoji.

Smiling, Misty texted her back and was just about to place her foot back on the pedal when she thought she heard something. She glanced over her shoulder, expecting to see a jogger or biker coming up behind her, but there was no one there. Frowning, she stood completely still and listened as she slowly took in her surroundings once again. The trail was shaded and full of shadows as the sun continued to hide behind dull, gray clouds, and a cold breeze rustled the many trees and bushes that surrounded the lake. Misty shivered slightly as a chill of foreboding crept up her spine, and she suddenly had the feeling she shouldn't be riding around the lake by herself. Even if someone pulled into the parking lot, they wouldn't be able to come to her assistance quickly if she called out for help.

You're letting your imagination run away with you, she told herself. *There's no one here but you, the squirrels, and a few ducks.*

With a sigh, Misty shook her head and continued on her way, only a bit faster this time. She'd just made it to the halfway point when her cellphone chimed once again, alerting her to Tori's arrival. Peering through the trees, she could see her friend's car pulling into the parking lot, and she quickened her pace.

Misty drew closer and closer to the bend in the road where, once rounded, she would have a straight shot to the parking area. Suddenly, she heard the rev of an engine from behind and turned to see a dark motorcycle emerging from the trees. Dressed all in black, the driver wore a helmet, blocking any view of his or her face, and Misty realized with a catch of her breath that the motorcycle was coming directly toward her.

Turning back to face the trail, Misty pedaled faster, her heart pounding as her legs quickly started to burn from the exertion. She could hear the motorcycle drawing closer, and although she didn't know who it was, she knew in her heart that he or she meant to do her harm.

The bend in the trail was only a few feet away. If she could only reach it in time, maybe Tori would see her and be able to help somehow. The cold wind slapped angrily at her cheeks and burned her eyes, and she felt wet tears sliding quickly down her cheeks. Glancing back once again, she saw with a gasp that the motorcycle was only a few feet away, and with a quick thrust of a foot against the gas pedal, it jerked and shot toward her like a rocket.

Through a thick haze of fear, Misty felt the motorcycle connect with her bike. With a loud *crack,* she was sent flying over the handlebars and onto the steep hill just to the left of the trail. As soon as she hit the hard earth, the breath was knocked from her lungs. She tumbled uncontrollably down the incline as the world quickly became a blurred, jumbled mess of trees, bushes, grass, dirt, and gray skies. Unable to catch herself, Misty struck her head on a rock and was thrown into the freezing lake with a loud *splash.* Knocked unconscious, her eyes fluttered closed, and she quickly disappeared beneath the black, rippling surface.

Hearing the sound of a revving engine, Tori peered across the lake and through the trees, trying to find where the sound was coming from. Suddenly, a flash of aqua blue and bright coral caught her attention, and Tori's eyes widened in horror as she realized Misty was about to be shoved off the trail by a black motorcycle that was quickly bearing down on her.

Realizing her friend needed help, Tori jumped back into her car and jerked it into drive, her tires squealing as she raced across the parking lot toward the trail. Just as she entered the shaded path that was never intended for vehicles, she saw the motorcycle hit Misty and watched in horror as her friend tumbled down the hill and into the lake. Her heart pounding, Tori pressed the gas harder as trees and bushes flew by in a blur of green and brown. The motorcyclist veered off the trail and zoomed past her, but all she could see was the rippling of the water where Misty had gone under and had yet to surface.

Slamming on her brakes, Tori leaped from her car and raced to the water's edge, where she dove in without a second thought. The frigid lake took her breath away for a split second, but Tori was used to swimming in the cold water; she and Brice and their school friends used to sneak here during the winter months and would bet on who could stay in the water the longest.

Tori peered through the murky depths, her eyes burning as she searched for her friend. Just as a feeling of desperation threatened to overtake her, she spotted Misty floating lifelessly in the dark water only a few feet away. Swimming toward her with renewed vigor, Tori grabbed her friend by the arm and tugged upward. She'd been underwater for over thirty seconds, and her lungs were screaming for air as stars floated before her eyes.

Don't give up, she told herself as she searched

for the surface. ***You're almost there.***

Just when she thought she might black out, Tori broke through the rippling surface and gasped for air, her head spinning as she pulled Misty above the water and swam for the shore. By the time they made it, Tori was weak and out of breath, but she knew she couldn't waste any time resting. Lying Misty on her back, she began performing CPR as tears of fear filled her eyes. What if it was too late? What if Misty was already dead? She'd been in the water for over a minute and wasn't responsive. Desperately wishing that someone was there to help, Tori fought the feeling of panic that nearly blinded her.

Suddenly, Misty began to cough, and Tori turned her friend's head to the side so she wouldn't choke on the water that spewed from her mouth. Her face was as white as a ghost, and when she opened her beautiful gray eyes to stare up at her friend, Tori burst into tears and whispered, "Thank God."

CHAPTER 9

Misty lay shivering on the muddy bank and waited as Tori ran to her car to call for help. She was so weak she could barely turn her head, and all she wanted was to be at home, curled up in her nice warm bed with Wally at her side.

"The police and an ambulance will be here shortly," Tori said when she returned, her voice trembling. She'd brought a raincoat from her trunk and wrapped it tightly around Misty's shivering form, and they both sighed with relief when they heard the sound of sirens minutes later.

As soon as the paramedics arrived, Misty was hoisted onto a gurney, carried to an awaiting ambulance, and taken to the small, nearby hospital where the doctor on call would determine whether she should be transported to Savannah. The heated blanket the paramedics wrapped her in felt like a piece of Heaven, and while they checked her vitals and discussed her condition on the way to the hospital, she found herself drifting off to sleep.

The next hour was a blur. Upon her arrival at the hospital, the doctor gave her a careful and thorough examination before determining that her lungs looked clear.

"Although you were submerged for well over a minute," he told Misty, "it seems the cold temperature stunned you to the point that you only swallowed a bit of water, and with Ms. Barlow's quick action, your life was spared. You do, however," he added, peering over his glasses at her, "have a couple of bruised ribs, a nasty cut on your forehead, a slight concussion, and a sprained wrist. You'll need to rest and take it easy for at least a couple of weeks."

The way he looked at her made Misty wonder how he knew she wasn't the type to "take it easy". She had so much work to do on the house, plus all of her plans to uncover more about her past; how was she going to just sit idly by and "rest" for two weeks? Just the thought of it made her feel worse than she already felt.

After giving her some medication and a few additional instructions, the doctor told Misty she could go home, and a nurse wheeled her out into the waiting area where Tori, her parents, and Brice were gathered.

"How are you feeling, honey?" Mrs. Amy asked, her brow wrinkled with concern.

"Ready to get into my bed, snuggle up with Wally, and sleep for hours," Misty replied with a tired smile.

"You can definitely do that, only it'll be at *my* house," Tori stated.

"Tori, you have too much going on at the coffee

shop to be bothered with me…" Misty started to protest, but was interrupted when Mrs. Amy spoke up once again.

"Why don't you both come to stay at our house?" she asked. "Neil has to go out of town later this afternoon for a horse auction and will be gone until Saturday, so I'd love to have the company. We can have some much needed girl time."

"My plumber said he won't be able to fix my toilet until Friday afternoon, so that works for me," Tori said with an excited clap.

"You can ride with us, while Tori and Brice go to your house to pick up Wally and anything you may need," Mrs. Amy added, volunteering her nephew's services without asking.

Knowing better than to argue, and not possessing the strength to do so anyway, Misty nodded her head in agreement. As they left the hospital, with Brice pushing her wheelchair, Tori told Misty that Officer Lewis wanted to talk to her.

"Officer Dylan Mitchell, his partner, already questioned me," she stated, "but he said that Officer Lewis will want to talk to you tomorrow when he gets back on duty."

They'd just made it to Mrs. Amy's car when Brice finally spoke up. "I can't believe someone did this to you," he said. He bent over to help Misty stand up, his blue eyes filled with concern. "Misty, you could have been killed."

His face was very close to hers, and it warmed Misty's heart over how upset he was.

"But thanks to your cousin's quick action and lightning reflexes, I'm here to see the light of another day," she replied with a smile.

"I always made certain she was a good swimmer," Mr. Neil stated proudly.

"But who would do something like this?" Mrs. Amy asked, her voice choked as tears filled her eyes. "They *both* could have been killed, while whoever was responsible just ran off in the opposite direction."

"Did you see who it was, Misty?" Brice asked as Misty got settled in the back seat.

"No," Misty replied, shaking her head. "A helmet covered all discernable features."

"That's what I told Officer Mitchell," Tori said with a sigh.

After giving Tori a list of everything she and Wally would need, Misty rode with Mr. and Mrs. Barlow to their home. Once they arrived at the beautiful 45-acre horse ranch, Mr. Neil helped Misty into the house while Mrs. Amy rushed upstairs to "fix up" the guest bedroom.

"Is there anything you need?" Mr. Neil kindly asked Misty as she sank down onto the soft, plush sofa in the living room.

"No, thank you," she replied, smiling gratefully when he grabbed a nearby afghan and wrapped it around her shoulders.

As he went upstairs to help his wife, Misty curled up against the sofa and soon drifted off to sleep. Her body was aching and exhausted, but her mind was tortured over the events of the day and a dream quickly began to take form. She was riding her bike around the lake once again, but it was as if she was standing outside of herself, watching everything unfold from afar. She knew that danger lurked in those dark woods, ready to pounce, and she tried to scream out a warning but couldn't seem to utter any sound past her swollen throat.

Beads of sweat gathered on Misty's brow, and she struggled to awaken, but couldn't. Her legs began to cramp and burn, and her heart raced wildly within her chest. Just then, she heard the rev of an engine and saw the motorcycle race from the trees and head right toward her. It drew closer and closer while she stood frozen in place, watching herself pedal a bicycle that wasn't moving. She could see the lake and knew that it was only a matter of seconds until she felt its cold, icy hands surrounding her and pulling her further and further under.

Misty didn't hear the front door open, nor did she sense his presence standing over her in the Barlow's living room. She lay there, helplessly trapped within the confines of her dream, and when he touched her arm, she thought that her heart was going to explode.

Gasping, Misty's eyes flew open and she quickly sat up, only to grab both her head and stomach and fall back against the sofa cushions with a groan of pain.

"Misty, are you alright?"

Brice sat beside her, his eyes full of worry as he reached out to take her hand.

"Y-yes, I'm fine," she nodded. Leaning her head back, she took a deep breath, trying to slow the racing of her heart. "I was having a bad dream and didn't hear anyone walk into the room, so you startled me," she explained after a moment. "Thanks for waking me, though; I was about to take my second tumble into Lake Laurier."

"One tumble is enough," he said, squeezing her hand gently. "You had me pretty worried."

Hearing the concern in his voice, Misty raised her head to look at Brice. "Oh yeah?" she asked.

His eyes warm, Brice nodded. "Yeah. You need to be more careful, Misty."

Their faces were only inches apart, and he was staring at her so intently that Misty felt her cheeks begin to flush. When he reached up to tuck a strand of hair behind her ear, she felt warm and confused and a little dizzy, but before she could get her thoughts to make any sense, the front door opened and Misty heard the sound of panting and the tapping of toenails against the hardwood floor.

With a twinkle in her eye, Misty slid further down onto the soda and let out a soft whistle, grinning when she heard Wally take off through the house in her direction. It wasn't long before he found her, and with bright eyes, he lunged at her head and covered her with wet, slobbery kisses.

"Brice, where did you go?" Tori yelled from the foyer. "You need to take Misty's suitcase upstairs."

"My C.O. calls," Brice stated with a roll of his eyes, and Misty chuckled as he hurried back through the house to help Tori.

Mrs. Amy and Mr. Neil came back down the stairs with an armload of bedsheets, and Misty asked, "Are y'all sure it's okay for Wally to be here? I don't want him to be an inconvenience. He can stay in the barn if he needs to."

"Oh, honey, we're used to having animals in the house," Mrs. Amy said as she came over to rub Wally's ears. "Ever since Tori was seven, she brought one animal after another home to be taken care of."

"Yeah, remember the foal?" Mr. Neil spoke up, shaking his head.

With a laugh, Mrs. Amy nodded and said, "Oh my, yes." Looking at Misty, she explained, "One of our horses died during birth, and when December rolled around, we had a freezing spell pass through. Tori insisted we keep the foal in the kitchen because it was too cold to be left in the barn."

"But isn't the barn climate controlled?" Misty asked, her lips twitching.

"It is," Tori spoke up as she and Brice entered the room. "But I distinctly remember a storm was coming through that night and it was possible that our electricity would go out. I just couldn't stand to think of that poor, sweet baby shivering out in the barn all night."

Misty burst into laughter, but quickly regretted the action when her head began to pound. Reaching up to grab her temples, Misty scrunched up her face and moaned.

"It's time for you to go upstairs and get some rest," Mrs. Amy stated. "I'll bring you a couple of icepacks as soon as you get settled."

Tori and Wally led the way while Brice helped Misty up the stairs, and before long, Misty was snuggled between the covers, promising to let someone know if she needed anything. All her life, she'd had to take care of herself with no one to worry or fret over her. Being all alone in the world had never been easy, and Misty was so grateful to have the Barlow's in her life now.

That night, Misty lay in the dark, unfamiliar room with her arm wrapped firmly around Wally as she thought about the events of the day. Why would anyone want to hurt her? She'd simply asked a few questions about something that happened twenty-five years ago. Apparently, someone had a secret they didn't want to be uncovered, and she had a feeling it had something to do with what she'd discovered in those newspaper clippings in her closet.

Just then, Luxton O'Reilly's visit to her house floated through her mind, and the way he'd all but threatened her sent chills up her spine. Perhaps she'd gotten in over her head this time. What would happen once she was well and could return home? Would someone try to hurt her again?

CHAPTER 10

The next morning, Misty woke to the smell of a home cooked breakfast, and with a rumbling stomach, she slowly and carefully made her way down the stairs. Her ribs were extremely sore and her wrist swollen, but she was thankful to be alive. Wally pranced along beside her, and when they entered the kitchen, Misty found Tori and Mrs. Amy buzzing around the kitchen like two little bees.

"Something smells amazing," Misty said as she walked to the back door to let Wally outside.

"Oh, Misty, I'll let him out," Tori said as soon as she saw her friend. "You go sit down."

Misty sank gratefully down into one of the barstools at the counter and looked over at Mrs. Amy to find that the older woman was eyeing her closely.

"You look pale, honey," she stated with concern. "How are you feeling?"

"Sore and stiff, but okay," Misty replied with a smile. "Did Mr. Neil make it to Hazelhurst last night?"

Mrs. Amy nodded. "Yes, he did," she replied. She then proceeded to place a plate on the counter before Misty and piled it high with biscuits and gravy, bacon, and scrambled eggs.

As the women ate the delicious breakfast, they discussed what happened the day before, chatted about local gossip, and talked of their plans for Christmas. Mrs. Amy and Tori asked Misty to join them for their family Christmas dinner, and Misty readily agreed. She'd spent Thanksgiving with them, and couldn't wait to discover how much fun Christmas would be. Mrs. Amy had the house decorated beautifully with a homemade wreath on the front door, a massive, sparkling Christmas tree in the living room, garland on the mantle, and vintage carolers standing by the fireplace. She'd even decorated the kitchen with a Santa Claus tablecloth, tiny Christmas tree salt and pepper shakers, and a poinsettia on the table. Since there were still so many renovations left to do in her house, Misty hadn't been able to do any decorating this year, but she was excited to give it a go next Christmas.

After breakfast, the three women piled up on the sofa and watched *It's A Wonderful Life,* and then right after lunch, Tori announced she had to run to her house.

"I can't remember if I turned the heat down or not, and it's driving me crazy," she said with a sigh. "Do you need anything from your house, Misty?"

Misty shook her head, and Mrs. Amy said, "Would you mind stopping by the market to pick up some lettuce for supper? I'm making spaghetti, and you always need salad with spaghetti. Oh, and also bread because we'll need garlic toast. Oh, and…"

Laughing, Tori said, "Why don't you just come with me? I can drop you at the market while I run home."

Looking over at Misty, Mrs. Amy asked, "Will you be okay here by yourself for a little while? We won't be long, I promise."

With a smile, Misty nodded and assured them both that she would be just fine. After they left, she leaned back against the sofa and did the breathing exercises the doctor told her to do so pneumonia wouldn't set in, and after a bit, she drifted off to sleep with Wally at her side. She'd only dozed a few moments when she suddenly jerked awake, her heart pounding, and she glanced quickly around the room in search of what had awakened her. Just then, she realized Wally was standing up, his tail down, and a low growl emanated from his throat as he faced the front of the house. Sitting up straight, Misty ignored the pain in her stomach as she looked in that direction and wondered if someone was outside.

With a grimace, Misty pushed herself up and walked slowly toward the foyer, her ears listening intently for any sound coming from the front porch. If someone was there, why didn't they ring the doorbell? Just as she entered the foyer, Misty stopped and felt a cold chill sweep over her.

Perhaps whoever tried to kill her yesterday was back to finish the job. Perhaps they'd been watching and knew she was all alone in the house, with no security system and no close neighbors to help.

Feeling the pockets of her pajama pants, Misty realized she'd left her cellphone upstairs. With a sigh, she turned to make her way back through the house, but stopped in her tracks when she suddenly heard the sound of humming. Her brow furrowing, Misty listened to the deep, guttural sounds coming from the other side of the front door and felt her body go tense with fear.

Just then, the doorknob jiggled slightly, and Misty gasped, her heart pounding. He was trying to get in, and she suddenly realized that Tori hadn't locked the kitchen door when she let Wally inside earlier that morning. Whoever was out there could simply run around to the back of the house and be inside before Misty could make it upstairs to her cellphone.

"Hello? Is anyone home?"

Misty jerked as the deep, familiar voice rang out, and with a breath of relief, she opened the front door to find Officer Lewis standing on the other side.

"Officer Lewis, it's you," she said in a breathless tone. "You scared me."

His head tilting in confusion, Officer Lewis pointed to the doorbell and said, "I rang the bell."

"Oh," Misty replied with a sheepish laugh. "I

was dozing on the sofa and I guess I didn't hear it."

Just then, Misty noticed Tori's car coming down the long driveway, and she threw her hand up in a wave, wondering why they were back so soon.

"I forgot my purse," Mrs. Amy explained as she jumped from the car and hurried into the house. Nodding at Officer Lewis, she smiled and said, "Good afternoon, Harlem."

Officer Lewis walked inside with the two women and followed Misty into the living room, where they both sat. Wally took his place next to his owner as he eyed their visitor suspiciously, and Misty kept her hand on his collar in case he decided he didn't like cops.

"I'm sure you're not feeling well, Miss Raven, so I won't take much of your time," Officer Lewis stated as he pulled a pen and notepad from his shirt pocket. "I read Miss Barlow's statement that she gave Dylan, my partner, and now I'd like to hear your side of the story."

Mrs. Amy waved goodbye to the two of them as she hurried from the house, and Misty took a deep breath, as if trying to gain enough strength to relay the whole ugly story. As she spoke, her skin began crawling as chills swept over her body. She wrapped her sweater tighter around herself and pulled the Afghan from the back of the sofa to tuck securely around her legs.

"I know he was wearing a helmet, and Miss Barlow said there was no license plate on the

91

motorcycle, but did you notice anything familiar about the man's appearance?" Officer Lewis asked.

"I honestly couldn't say if it was a man or woman," Misty said with a sigh. "Everything happened so fast that I couldn't get a good look at who was driving the motorcycle."

"I see," Officer Lewis replied, chewing on his bottom lip as he thought. "You know, I believe Luxton O'Reilly owns a motorcycle, so I'll check with him first and go from there. If you think of anything, please let me know."

After a brief hesitation, Misty told Officer Lewis about Luxton O'Reilly's visit to her house and how threatened she'd felt.

His brow lowering, Officer Lewis asked, "Why didn't you tell me about this sooner?"

"I didn't want to cause more trouble," she replied, sighing.

Eyeing her with a raised eyebrow, he said, "Well, if anything like that happens again, please let me know immediately."

Misty nodded. "Yes, I will."

Misty stood to walk him out, but he held up his hand and said, "No, you stay put; I'll see myself out. I hope you feel better soon, and I also hope this has taught you a lesson to stay out of other people's business. You were almost killed, Miss Raven; I'd say you should take that pretty seriously."

Pursing her lips stubbornly, Misty smiled tightly

and, ignoring his statement, asked, "Will you let me know if you find anything?"

With a heavy sigh, Officer Lewis nodded and left without another word. After he was gone, Misty went upstairs to get her cellphone, not wishing to be in the house alone without it. When she unlocked the screen, she saw a missed call and text message from Adam.

"I heard about what happened," he wrote. *"Are you alright? I've been so worried."*

Smiling at his concern, Misty returned his text as she went back downstairs, assuring him she was fine.

"A little banged up and bruised, but I've always healed quickly," she said.

They continued to text, and as Misty settled back down onto the sofa and waited for his responses, her thoughts went back to her conversation with Officer Lewis. He'd said that Luxton O'Reilly owned a motorcycle, but would he be so careless as to come to her house, threaten her, and then two days later make good on that threat? After remembering the cold look in his eyes, however, when he stood on her front porch and warned her to stay out of their business, Misty knew she wouldn't be surprised if he was the one responsible for running her off the road.

CHAPTER 11

The next morning, Misty felt even more sore than the day before and could barely pull herself out of bed. After getting dressed, she slowly and carefully made her way downstairs and into the kitchen, where she asked Tori to let Wally outside.

"I need to eat something and take my pain medication," she told her friend.

Mrs. Amy was sitting at the kitchen table sipping on a cup of coffee and reading the newspaper, but as soon as she saw how pale Misty was, she jumped to her feet and helped Misty sit down.

"I'll fix you some grits and toast," she said, hurrying around to the pantry to grab the needed ingredients.

"After I let Wally out, I'll get you some coffee," Tori stated as she eyed her friend with concern.

Tori opened the back door for Wally, and he'd barely stepped outside when, suddenly, he let out a loud yelp of pain. Her eyes widening, Tori ran out the door to check on him and, ignoring the pain and swirling in her head, Misty pushed herself up and quickly followed Mrs. Amy outside.

"What happened?" Misty gasped when she saw

Wally holding up a paw that was dripping with blood.

"There's glass all over the porch," Tori said in a bewildered tone as she kneeled next to Wally. "He's got a nasty cut, Misty. I'd better take him to the vet immediately."

"Where on earth did all of this glass come from?" Mrs. Amy cried.

Tori pointed to what appeared to be the lid to a jar resting a few feet away by the porch steps and asked, "Isn't that the jar you use to scoop bird seed out of the bag?"

"It could be," Mrs. Amy replied, looking about with frazzled eyes. "I guess a raccoon or something knocked it over in the night. Misty, I'm so sorry."

"It's not your fault, Mrs. Amy," Misty said as she slowly kneeled beside her pet. He looked so pitiful with his large, sad eyes, and the way he held his foot up and whimpered nearly broke Misty's heart.

Tori ran around the side of the house to retrieve her car, and when she returned and began coercing Wally into the back seat, Misty stated she was going with them. After helping Wally limp into the car, Misty climbed in beside him and the three women headed for the vet.

"I don't understand why none of us heard that jar break last night," Tori commented as she turned from their driveway onto the main road.

"Wally woke me up a little after eleven o'clock

last night," Misty said as she gently rubbed the top of his head, which rested in her lap. "He was up and pacing around the room; I wonder if maybe he heard something."

"Those pesky raccoons," Mrs. Amy said with a sigh. "I'll make sure to never leave anything breakable out there again. Oh," she added, leaning down to retrieve something from her purse, "I grabbed your pain medicine, a bottle of water, and a banana as I was running out the door, Misty."

Breathing a sigh of relief, Misty took the items and said, "You're the best, Mrs. Amy."

"She always thinks of everything," Tori stated, smiling warmly at her mother.

Misty had never experienced the love and care that can only come from a true mother; at least, not that she could remember, and the fact that Mrs. Amy had been so kind and thoughtful warmed Misty's heart.

They arrived at the vet in record time, and Misty eased herself slowly from the car as Tori helped Wally out of the back seat. The towel Misty had wrapped around his foot was soaked in blood, and her stomach clenched with worry as they helped him walk inside.

"Goodness, what a big fellow!" a loud voice exclaimed as soon as they entered the small clinic, and Misty looked up to see a redheaded woman in her fifties hurrying their way. She wore a white lab coat over a florescent pink sweater, and a pair of black horn-rimmed glasses perched on the edge of her nose.

"Hi, Mrs. Kirby," Tori greeted the older woman. "This is Wally, and he has a very bad cut on his paw from stepping on some broken glass."

Pushing her lower lip out into an "I'm so sorry" pout, Mrs. Kirby motioned toward one of the back rooms and asked that they take him inside. As they walked back, the veterinarian's name suddenly sunk in, and she glanced at Mrs. Kirby curiously.

"Are you related to Principal Glenn Kirby?" she asked as they entered the small examination room.

"Why, yes, I'm his wife," the woman beamed. "And who might you be, honey?"

"Kyra, this is Misty Raven," Mrs. Amy spoke up. "She's the one who.. "

"Is searching for her mother," Kyra interrupted with a nod. Smiling at Misty, she reached out to pat her hand and said, "I've heard all about you."

"I was going to say she's the one who bought the old bed-and-breakfast," Mrs. Amy stated with a cocked eyebrow and a slightly annoyed expression at being interrupted.

"Oh, yes, I knew that, too," Kyra stated, waving her hand in the air. Looking down at Wally, she kneeled to take a look at his paw and, after a close examination, said, "You were right, Tori; this is a very bad cut and is going to need stitches. He's also lost a good bit of blood, the poor dear."

Misty's stomach dropped. "He…he's going to be okay, though, right?"

Standing to her full height, Kyra nodded and

said, "Oh, yes, he'll be just fine. He'll have to wear a cone for about a week, and I would really like to monitor him overnight, just to make sure the stitches don't come loose and his foot doesn't start bleeding again."

Bending to pat her sweet boy on the head, Misty said softly, "Yes, ma'am, that will be fine."

Wally let out a low whine and nudged Misty's hand, and she felt tears pop into her eyes. How had she come to love this animal so much? She'd never had a pet before and had only gotten Wally a couple of months ago, but their bond was already so strong that Misty couldn't imagine her life without him.

"Be a good boy, and I'll see you tomorrow," Misty whispered, kissing Wally on the head as Kyra's assistant led him to the back to stitch up his wound. He looked so sad, and Misty wondered if he was remembering the time he'd spent locked away at the animal shelter. She only hoped he didn't think she was sending him back there.

Kyra walked the ladies out, and as Misty fished around her purse for her credit card, she listened as the older woman rattled on nonstop.

"Amy, you and Neil need to come over one night soon and have supper with us," she was saying. "I wish you could have been there last night; I made a new baked chicken recipe, and it was to die for! Glenn didn't get any, though; he had a meeting after work and didn't get home until almost midnight. I told him this morning that he's in the doghouse! Sorry," she giggled, elbowing Mrs. Amy, "I tend to make a lot of animal jokes. Occupational hazard, I guess."

After paying the bill and agreeing to pick Wally up the following morning, the three women told Kyra goodbye and left the vet clinic. Just as they were stepping outside, Patrick Donovan was walking toward them with a Basset Hound following slowly along beside him.

"Hello, ladies," he greeted them with a friendly smile. "Is one of the horses sick?"

"No, Misty's dog cut his paw, so we brought him in to get stitches," Tori explained, motioning toward Misty. "He's going to have to stay overnight, the poor thing."

Raising his eyebrows sympathetically, Patrick looked at Misty to offer his condolences, but stopped when he saw how pale she was and the bruise on her forehead. "Goodness, Miss Raven, you should be at home resting," he exclaimed. Reaching out to touch her arm, he asked, "How are you feeling? I heard about the accident."

Smiling wanly, Misty replied, "I'm alright; thank you for asking. I'd feel a lot better if Wally could come home with me today, though. I hate leaving him here overnight."

Nodding his head in understanding, Patrick said, "I know what you mean. Mr. Chewie here has had an upset stomach for a few days, so I'm afraid he'll be spending the night here as well."

Bending slowly, Misty patted Mr. Chewie on the

head and said, "Keep Wally company, okay? And make sure he behaves."

Mr. Chewie stared up at Misty with a disinterested look, and when he suddenly belched loudly, Misty couldn't help but giggle.

"I'd better get him inside before he gets sick again and ruins your shoes," Patrick chuckled. Nodding to the three women, he said, "I'll be seeing you."

They waved goodbye and headed for Tori's car when Patrick called out, "Amy, when is Neil getting back from the auction? I need to talk to him about something."

Glancing at Patrick with a wrinkled brow, as if surprised that he knew her husband was away, Mrs. Amy said, "He'll be back tomorrow afternoon."

Nodding, Patrick smiled and waved before disappearing inside the clinic.

After climbing into Tori's car, Mrs. Amy said, "I didn't realize anyone knew Neil was gone. Oh, well, Brice or Pops must have told someone at the store."

As they drove away from the vet, Misty sighed and leaned her head back against the headrest. She missed Wally already, and hoped he'd do well in the night and really be able to come home the next morning.

CHAPTER 12

That night, the three women made homemade hot chocolate and watched *Holiday Affair* with Robert Mitchum and Janet Leigh. Misty loved old movies; she used to watch them often with her dear old neighbor, Mr. Sikes, who always said they made him think of his younger years. Oh, how she missed that man; he'd been the only person who'd seemed like family to her when she was growing up.

"Family isn't always blood, Misty," he'd told her once. *"We can find family in a coworker, schoolteacher, or even a wrinkled up old neighbor. It's about finding those few special people who are kindred spirits."*

As his words floated through her mind, Misty glanced around the living room at Tori and Mrs. Amy and smiled softly, feeling thankful to have found a family here in Shady Pines.

Once the movie was finished, Misty took her pain medicine and went to bed. As she curled up between the covers, she missed having Wally beside her and hoped he was doing okay at the vet. She was planning to go home tomorrow and wanted to take him with her.

Misty fell asleep at a little past ten o'clock, and just before midnight, her eyes popped open and she sat up in bed. The room was dark and quiet as she looked around, but something had roused her; what was it?

Just then, the sound of distant thunder rattled the window panes, and Misty realized the culprit must be a storm that was apparently rolling in. She started to lie back down when, suddenly, the sound of footsteps out in the hallway met her ears. Her brow furrowing, Misty slowly climbed from bed and tiptoed toward the door. Had the storm awakened Tori and Mrs. Amy, too? She'd barely made it halfway across the room when her door suddenly began to open. Her eyes widening, Misty stopped and waited to see who was on the other side.

"Misty, are you awake?" a voice whispered in the darkness.

Releasing the breath she hadn't realized she was holding, Misty said, "Yes, I'm awake. Tori, why are you up wandering around so late?"

Tori stepped further into the room, and from the glow of the cellphone she was carrying, Misty could see the look of fear on her friend's face. "I thought I heard something downstairs a few minutes ago," she said, gripping Misty's arm tightly. "Isn't that why you're up?"

"Well, something *did* wake me, but I thought it was the storm," Misty replied, keeping her voice low. "What did you hear? It's not your mom, is it?"

"No, it wasn't me," Mrs. Amy stated from the doorway, and both girls gasped in surprise.

"Good grief, Mom!" Tori exclaimed breathlessly as she grabbed her chest. "Warn a person before sneaking up on them like that."

"Why are you up, Mrs. Amy?" Misty asked. "Did you hear something, too?"

Mrs. Amy nodded, her eyes worried. "It almost sounded like someone was trying to get in the back door."

"Should we call the police?" Misty asked.

Suddenly, a loud *thump* sounded downstairs, and Tori hurried across the bedroom to grab a long, jade figurine her grandfather had brought back from Vietnam. "By the time the police get here, we could all be dead," she hissed. "I'm going downstairs."

Misty and Mrs. Amy followed Tori out into the hallway, their hearts racing and fingers tense as they clutched the handrail and inched quietly down the stairs. The house was dark, and the storm was drawing closer. Misty could hear the wind getting stronger as it whistled through the trees and beat softly against the house, and they could see random flashes of lightning coming through the windows in the living room just below. Misty desperately wished for Wally's comforting presence, and the thought that his accident with the glass may not have been an accident after all suddenly flashed through her mind. Had someone purposefully planted that glass on the back porch hoping Wally would get hurt and wouldn't be around that night to protect them?

They finally reached the living room and stood in a tight, close line as they listened, their ears trained toward the kitchen. The ***thump*** they'd heard before kept randomly repeating itself, and Misty's stomach clenched with fear as they began moving as one in that direction. Tori held the figurine tightly in her hand, ready to strike, when the door to the kitchen was suddenly flung open and all three women jumped back and screamed in unison.

Mrs. Amy was the first to speak. "Oh, for goodness' sake," she said with a nervous chuckle. "It looks like the back door was blown open by the wind; we must not have closed it tightly when we left the house with Wally this morning."

Shaking her head, she flipped on the lights and hurried through the kitchen to grab the flapping door and push it closed, making certain to turn the lock. Misty stood uncertainly in the doorway and looked around while Tori checked the pantry with her weapon poised to strike.

"I don't see anyone," Tori said, sighing with relief. Looking at Misty, she added in a sheepish tone, "I guess we're still a little shaken up after what happened at the lake."

Trying to ignoring her throbbing wrist and ribs, Misty nodded and said, "I guess so."

They'd just turned off the kitchen lights and

were about to head back up the stairs when the sound of footsteps on the porch and a key jiggling the lock on the front door met their ears. With a gasp, they hurried through the house just as the front door swung open and Mr. Neil stepped in.

When he saw them, his eyes widened in surprise and he said, "What are you three doing up so late? And Tori, what on earth are you doing with that old figurine? You look like you're about to clobber me with it."

"Neil, you scared us half to death!" Mrs. Amy exclaimed, placing her hands on her hips. "What are you doing here tonight? You're not supposed to be back until tomorrow."

Shrugging, he smiled and said, "I wanted to come home early. I didn't mean to wake up the entire house, though."

"You didn't wake us up," Tori said, stepping forward to kiss him on the cheek. "The back door did."

As Tori and Mrs. Amy explained what happened, Misty couldn't help but wonder if that was, in fact, really what happened. It seemed awfully strange that Wally stepped on broken glass, which mysteriously appeared on the back porch, and then the back door just "happened" to come open by itself in the middle of the night. Shivering slightly, Misty rubbed her arms and tried to ward off the feeling of foreboding that crept up her spine. Had someone been trying to break into the house, but was scared off by Mr.

Neil's unexpected arrival? She couldn't be certain, but after they'd all said their good nights once again and Misty climbed back into her bed a bit later, she was thankful that Mr. Neil decided to come home early.

CHAPTER 13

The next morning, Misty and Tori packed up their things and, after Misty thanked the family for their kindness and hospitality, climbed into Tori's car and headed to the vet.

"Are you sure you feel up to staying on your own?" Tori asked as they drove. "Because if you don't, you and Wally are more than welcome to stay with me."

Misty smiled at her friend. "I think I'll be okay," she said. "Thank you for the invitation, though, and if I find I can't make it on my own, I'll let you know."

When they arrived at the vet, they went inside to find an empty waiting room. No one was at the front desk, and the place was so quiet that Misty wondered if the vet was closed and someone forgot to lock the front door.

Glancing over at Tori in confusion, Misty opened her mouth to say something, but stopped when she heard a voice coming from one of the back rooms. It sounded like Kyra Kirby, and she didn't sound very pleased.

"I don't understand why you were late getting home *again* last night," Kyra snapped, and Misty realized she must be on the phone. "I was willing to overlook it the night before, but now I'm starting to wonder…"

She stopped talking, and Misty and Tori shared a look. "Should we go out and come back in with a bit more noise, so she knows we're here?" Tori whispered.

"I don't want to hear excuses, Glenn," Kyra stated loudly. "I want to know where you were last night."

"Let's go back outside," Misty whispered in return, and the two women tiptoed back out the door.

"Do you think we should wait a bit before going back in?" Tori asked, her eyes wide.

"Or maybe we should keep listening, and then ask what his explanation was," Misty replied with a snicker.

Elbowing her friend lightly, Tori laughed and said, "You're terrible."

Before they could decide what to do, the front door opened and Kyra Kirby stuck her head out. "What on earth are y'all doing standing around out here?" she asked with a wide smile, her tone light. Her mascara was a bit smudged, as if she'd been crying, and it was obvious she was being forcibly cheerful.

"Oh, uh, we were just about to come inside," Tori replied with a bright smile of her own.

They followed Kyra back into the clinic, and Misty noticed a wrinkled up tissue sticking out of her coat pocket. Misty couldn't help but wonder why Principal Kirby was getting home so late at night and was curious what his response to his wife had been.

"Wally did very well in the night," Kyra said as she stepped behind the desk. "As I said before, he'll have to wear a cone for a while, but if you keep a close eye on him, I'm sure he'll be just fine."

"So, I can take him home?" Misty asked in a hopeful tone.

"Yes, yes, you certainly can," Kyra nodded exuberantly, her red bangs bouncing across her forehead.

"That's wonderful news," Misty replied with a sigh of relief.

While Kyra sent someone back to get Wally, Misty took the opportunity to ask her about Elena.

"When I was here yesterday, you said you'd heard of my search for information about my mother," she said. "Do you remember her, by chance?"

Kyra's cheerful, polite expression tightened slightly, and the smile that followed seemed a bit forced. "Yes, I do," she replied, glancing down at her bright red fingernails that she tapped lightly against the desk. "I'd say she was very hard to forget."

Misty blinked in surprise at Kyra's words; this was the first person who clearly seemed to remember Elena, while everyone else's memories were vague.

"You knew her pretty well then?" Misty asked in a hopeful tone.

Kyra cleared her throat and said, "Well, no, not really. I believe I only spoke to her once." At the look of confusion on Misty's face, she laughed slightly and added, "I only meant that Elena was so beautiful, it's hard to forget someone like that. All the men in town talked about her, including my beloved husband, but Elena was very standoffish. She was from another country, you know, and had quite a thick accent, so I don't think she made many friends in town. From what I remember, she and her husband kept to themselves."

Kyra's jaw clenched at the mention of Glenn and how the men in town talked about Elena, and Misty quickly brought the subject away from Elena and to herself.

"Do you remember if they had any children?" she asked.

Kyra didn't say anything for a moment; she simply stared down at her tapping fingernails in silence. Finally, she looked back up at Misty and, with a tight smile, said, "No, I don't remember."

The door that led to the kennels swung open just then, interrupting their conversation, and Wally was brought into the main room. His foot was bandaged, and he bumped the massive cone against every wall and door he passed. As soon as he spotted Misty, his tail began to wag, and he lunged toward her with a look of pure joy on his face.

"Hey, you," she greeted him with a smile as she gently rubbed his back. Looking up at Kyra, she said in a sincerely grateful tone, "Thank you so much for taking care of him, Kyra. It means so much to me."

"You're very welcome," she replied. Her cellphone rang then, and she waved goodbye and quickly hurried into the back room.

Tori helped Misty get Wally into the back seat of her car, and as they drove, Misty commented, "Kyra said that Elena mostly kept to herself, but Mr. Hendricks told me they had lunch together once."

"His wife also said it wasn't planned," Tori replied. "Mr. Hendricks is...well, the flirtatious sort, and I wouldn't put it past him to have pushed Elena into joining him for lunch."

"Did Kyra act a little odd to you when I asked if she remembered whether Elena and her husband had children?" Misty wanted to know.

Tori nodded as she turned into Misty's driveway. "Yes, very. Why do you think that is?"

"I don't know," Misty replied, sighing. "But I keep getting the feeling that people know more than they're saying."

Tori helped Misty and Wally into the house, made Misty promise to let her know if she needed anything, and then hugged her friend goodbye. As Misty watched Tori drive away, she found herself feeling uncomfortable for the first time at being left alone. After what happened at the lake, she was nervous and on edge, and the thought that someone was quite possibly trying to kill her made her rethink her decision not to stay with Tori.

This wasn't the first time someone has tried to kill you, she thought with a sigh as she set the security system and headed for the bedroom to change her clothes. ***You can't keep intruding on other people's lives; you've always done just fine taking care of yourself.***

Wally bumped her leg then with his extra large cone, and she smiled down at him.

"I'm not really alone, though, am I?" she said, reaching out to ruffle the fur at his shoulders. "You'll watch my back."

Although it was barely past noon, Misty was exhausted, and after changing into a pair of comfortable pajamas, she crawled into bed and went to sleep.

At three o'clock, Misty heard the doorbell ringing, and with bleary eyes, she stumbled out of bed and put her robe on. She hadn't intended to sleep so long, and as she headed through the house toward the front door, her stomach rumbled loudly.

When she reached the foyer, she paused uncertainly as images of Luxton O'Reilly's cold blue eyes and hard, threatening expression floated through her mind. Clearing her throat, she called out through the door, "Who is it?"

"Willow Ruis," a soft, airy voice responded. "I'm Stephanie's mother."

Her eyes widening in surprise, Misty quickly opened the door to find a very small and frail woman standing on the other side. She was terribly thin, with stringy brown hair and the most unusual eyes Misty had ever seen; they were a bluish-gray, and so light that they were almost translucent.

"I-I'm sorry if I'm disturbing you," Willow said, glancing uncertainly at Misty's rumpled robe and pajamas.

"Oh, no, you're not disturbing me," Misty assured her with a smile. "I was just taking a nap, but it was time I got up anyway. Would you like to come in?"

Nodding, Willow stepped into the house and quietly followed Misty into the living room, where they sat on the old, lumpy soda the previous owners had left behind. Misty had been planning to get new furniture as soon as the renovations were done, and hadn't expected to have company.

"Would you like something to drink?" Misty asked.

Willow shook her head. "No, thank you," she replied. Glancing down at her hands, which were clenched tightly in her lap, she said, "I heard that you think your mother may have been Elena Himmel, and that you're investigating the disappearances of my daughter and the other two girls."

She spoke so softly that Misty had to lean toward her to hear everything she was saying. "Yes, that's right," Misty said with a nod, wondering if perhaps Willow was going to ask her to stay out of it, just as Luxton O'Reilly had done. "Is that why you came to see me?"

Willow nodded, but didn't immediately speak. After a moment of silence, she slowly raised her head to look at her hostess, and the haunted look Misty saw in her eyes sent chills down her spine.

"Miss Raven," she finally said, her voice a bit louder this time and filled with a sense of urgency, "I…I think my daughter was murdered."

CHAPTER 14

Misty stared at Willow Ruis, shocked that one parent was willing to admit what may have really happened.

"Why do you think that?" Misty asked, tilting her head slightly as she studied the other woman.

"Because she was dating someone…well, I don't think they were "dating", but she liked him," Willow replied. "I know there's nothing odd about that, but she refused to tell anyone who he was; even Jessica and Tabitha."

Misty's brow furrowed, and she asked, "Why do you think she wouldn't tell anyone? And wouldn't Jessica and Tabitha have seen her talking to him at school?"

"I don't think he went to school with her, or at least not in the sense that you're referring to." Seeing the look of confusion on Misty's face, Willow leaned a bit closer and said, "I think he must have been older than her, and possibly even worked at the school."

Misty's eyes widened. "That would explain why she wouldn't share his identity," she said. "How did you find out about him?"

"I woke up late one night and went into the

kitchen to get something to drink," Willow replied. "I heard her talking on the phone, and when I stopped at her door to listen, she said that she loved him, too, and couldn't wait to be alone with him. When I asked her about it the next morning, she said it was just a boy from her class, but I saw that same boy a few days later with another girl. When I asked his mother about it, she told me they'd been dating for months. About a week after that, I found a bracelet on Stephanie's dresser with a heart and infinity sign clasped together; she said Tabitha and Jessica gave it to her."

"But you didn't believe her?"

Willow shook her head. "I saw Jessica at the market with her mother the next day and asked her about it; she said she'd never even seen the bracelet."

"Did you ever ask Tabitha or Jessica if Stephanie liked anyone?" Misty wanted to know.

"After Steph disappeared, I told the police about it and they spoke to Jessica and Tabitha. Both girls said that if Stephanie liked anyone, she never told them, and apparently they told each other everything." Willow paused and heaved a deep, heavy sigh, and her eyes filled with tears. "Everyone said she ran away because…because of me," she said in a choked whisper as she looked back down at her hands, "but when the other two girls disappeared shortly after, I knew my suspicions had to be correct."

Misty's forehead wrinkled slightly in confusion

as she listened to Willow's broken words. "What do you mean, Mrs. Ruis?" she asked. "Why did everyone think she ran away because of you?"

A tear dripped from her cheek and splashed against the threadbare jeans Willow wore, and she reached up with a shaky hand to wipe her face. "When Stephanie was about eight or nine, I began to deal with severe back pain," she said in a small, trembling voice. "The doctor said I had a herniated disc, and after the surgery, I…well, I became addicted to prescription drugs."

The guilt and pain Misty heard in Willow's voice broke her heart, and she reached across the distance to take her small, frail hand as a show of support. With a flinch of surprise, Willow slowly raised her eyes to stare at Misty, and the look of despair in their translucent depths made Misty want to cry.

"I struggled for years," she whispered. "I went to a couple of dry out clinics, but they only helped for so long. Finally, my husband had enough and left me, but he didn't take our daughter with him. I figured out later that he'd been wanting out for a long time, and my problem was his perfect excuse."

"You don't have to tell me all of this, Willow," Misty said gently.

Sniffing, Willow shook her head determinedly and said, "No, please, I want you to know everything that happened so that maybe you can help me finally find answers." Taking a deep breath, she wiped her eyes once again and continued. "After my husband left, I grew depressed, and that only worsened my condition. Stephanie came to hate me, and I hated myself; it was a vicious circle. I knew that this secret boyfriend was her idea of a way out, which is another reason I believe he was older and probably settled in a good job. He saw her need to escape and led her to believe he would marry her and save her from the prison she was living in. So, Miss Raven, I believe that because of me and my failure as a mother, my daughter was killed."

With the end of her story came a heaviness that seemed to settle on Willow's shoulders like a great weight, pressing her downward. She was crying, almost sobbing, and Misty wanted to wrap her arms around the small, frail woman and tell her it was going to be okay, but she couldn't; Willow's daughter was gone, and quite possibly never coming back. Life would never be completely "okay" again.

"Did the police look further into this secret boyfriend of Stephanie's?" Misty asked gently after walking into the kitchen to grab a box of tissues.

"No, they said there was nothing to go on," Willow replied, blowing her nose. "If I'm being completely honest, though, I don't think they believed me, and I guess…I guess I can't blame them."

Touching Willow lightly on the arm, Misty said,

"Well, *I* believe you, and I'd like to know if there's any additional information you can give me?"

Her eyes lighting up, Willow breathed a sigh of relief and said, "Thank you, Miss Raven; you do not know how much that means to me." Swiveling in her seat, Willow picked up her rather large purse from the floor and pulled out a large book. "This is the yearbook that was handed out in April, and Stephanie disappeared right before school ended in May," she explained, handing it to Misty. "I thought perhaps looking at the pictures might help you see something."

Opening the book, Misty slowly flipped through the pages, immediately noting the familiar faces she saw. Stephanie, Tabitha, and Jessica were always together, their young, happy smiles full of youthful energy and zest. Glenn Kirby was easy to find among the other teachers and even more handsome in his younger years. Misty was also a little surprised to even see a couple of photos with his wife, Kyra.

Flipping the page, Misty found yet another familiar face, and she pointed it out to Willow. "Is that Patrick Donovan?"

When Willow nodded "yes", Misty said, "I thought he worked at the elementary school during this time?"

"He did, but he was also the assistant coach for the boy's wrestling team at the high school."

"I didn't realize that," Misty muttered, wondering why he hadn't told her that when they talked before. Studying his picture, Misty was surprised at what an attractive young man he was. Tall and well built, with a head full of thick, dark hair, Patrick Donovan stared at the camera with his arms crossed and a charming, mischievous grin on his face.

Just then, Misty spotted Stephanie standing in the background of the photo, and she appeared to be talking to a young man with his back to the camera. She was smiling up at him, her head tilted flirtatiously, and Misty stared at the back of his head, thinking that he looked vaguely familiar.

"Willow, who is the young man Stephanie is talking to in this picture?" Misty asked, holding up the yearbook for Willow to see.

Leaning closer, her eyes squinting, Willow studied the photograph for a moment. Finally, she said, "I can't tell for certain, but I believe that's Walker Owens, her volleyball coach."

Misty blinked in surprise. "The man who owns Owens Security?"

Willow nodded. "That's right. He volunteered at the school for a few years while working at the police station, and then when he was about forty, he quit both jobs and started his own business."

"He installed my security system about a month ago," Misty stated. Flipping the pages until she found a better picture of him, her eyes widened at the tall, extremely muscular and good-looking man standing on the volleyball court, surrounded by his beaming, all-female team.

"It looks like I'll be paying a visit to Owens Security soon," she murmured under her breath. Another thought crossed her mind then when she saw a PTA photo of Huey and Darlene and a few other parents holding a t-shirt sale fundraiser. "Did the O'Reilly's also take part in the PTA?" she asked, pointing out the picture.

"I believe Catherine did, but I can't remember about her husband," Willow replied.

"So, were the parents at the school a good bit?"

Willow nodded. "Yes, if not for the PTA, then for an event; the school constantly had something going on."

Nodding, Misty smiled encouragingly and said, "Thank you so much for entrusting me with this, Willow. I'll do my best to find out what I can."

Her eyes filling with tears once again, Willow clutched Misty's hand and said in a choked voice, "Thank you so much. I can't tell you how good it feels to have someone believe me."

After Willow was gone, Misty couldn't stop thinking about their visit. What if she couldn't find anything? What if she had to tell Willow there was no hope of ever discovering what happened to her daughter? Willow was so fragile that Misty hated to think what would happen if she let her down.

I can't let that happen, she thought to herself as she went into her bedroom to let Wally out. *Whether or not I feel up to it yet, I'm paying a visit to Owens Security first thing Monday morning. I've got to find answers, and I've got to*

find them soon.

Noticing that her cellphone was lit up, Misty walked to her bedside table to see who was texting her. The message was from Brice, and he wanted to know how she and Wally were feeling.

"We're a pair," she replied with the bandaged emoji. *"But on the mend."*

"Good to hear," he said. *"I wouldn't want one of my favorite Shady Pines residents to stay down for long."*

Raising her eyebrows in surprise, Misty started to reply when his next text came through.

"I'm glad you're feeling better, too," he added with a wink emoji.

Grinning, Misty returned, *"I would say it hurts to laugh, but since your jokes aren't very funny, we don't have to worry about that."*

They continued with their banter as Misty slowly followed a limping Wally through the house and out the back door. He knocked his cone on every door, wall, and piece of furniture he passed, and she felt terrible that he had to wear the annoying contraption.

"If I knew you'd leave those stitches alone, I'd take that nasty cone off," she told him when he came back inside.

After fixing them both an early dinner, Misty cleaned up the kitchen and went back to her bedroom to take a shower and go to bed. When she opened her closet door and flipped on the light, however, something made her pause. Standing in the doorway with a feeling of confusion, she slowly looked around, wondering what seemed different. She'd always prided herself on being very organized and had a specific way of arranging her clothes and shoes, but something wasn't right.

Just then, she saw it; a random blue sweater was hanging in the middle of the greens, instead of beside them. It seemed it had fallen from its hanger and was put into the wrong place without thought, but Misty knew she hadn't done it. Or had she, and simply wasn't paying attention? Stepping further into the closet, something else caught her eye; the boxes on the top shelf where she kept her notes and newspaper clippings were moved and not stacked in the correct order. What was going on? Had the knock on her head been worse than the doctor thought?

Standing on her tiptoes, Misty pulled one box down and looked inside. She couldn't tell for certain, but it almost looked as if someone had rummaged through them. There were a few paperclips missing, and some dates weren't in the correct order. Was she imagining it, or had someone been in her house while she was staying at the Barlow's? If that was the case, she was glad she'd thought to put the most important articles in her safe.

Suddenly, Misty heard a creak over her head, and she looked up at the ceiling. The room above hers was a guest room, and even though the house constantly groaned and creaked, Misty's nerves were on edge and the thought that someone was walking around up there immediately flashed through her mind. Her heart pounding, she went to her bedside table and grabbed her Taser gun, her fingers trembling as she left Wally in the bedroom and headed upstairs.

The steps grunted beneath her feet as she slowly climbed upward, and her ears strained for the sound of footsteps or anything that would clue her in to the presence of another human being. She made it to the second floor and flipped on the lights, her body tense as adrenaline pulsed through her veins.

You should have just called the police, she told herself as she slowly made her way down the hallway toward the guest bedroom that rested just above hers. *You're too weak to fight anyone off; with or without a Taser.*

Misty could only imagine Officer Lewis's annoyance if she called him on a false alarm, and so she forced herself forward until she reached the guest bedroom. With a shaky hand, she turned the rattly old knob and pushed the door open, the Taser gun held out before her.

The door squeaked as it slowly opened, and Misty squinted at the shadows that seemed to leap toward her through the darkness. Random pieces of antique furniture with sheets draped across them dotted the room like ghosts waiting to pounce, and with quick, jerky movements, Misty flipped on the light switch, her eyes moving at lightning speed as she quickly surveyed the quiet area. No villains or intruders jumped out at her, and as she carefully made her way through the room, checking under the bed and in the closet, she realized with a feeling of both relief and foolishness that she'd simply let her imagination run away with her again.

As she made her way back downstairs, Misty still had the niggling feeling that someone had been in her closet, and then it suddenly hit her that Tori must have mussed things up a bit when she came by to get Misty's things. Feeling very silly for believing someone had broken into her house for the sole purpose of going through her closet, Misty shook her head and sighed.

Tori wouldn't have messed with the boxes on the top shelf, though, she thought, pausing at the bottom of the staircase.

If someone really had broken in, how could they have gotten in and out of her house without setting off the alarm? Perhaps Walker Owens used a generic code when he installed his security systems, and most people in town knew what it was.

Deciding that it was better to be safe than sorry, Misty went to the main keypad in the foyer and changed the code.

CHAPTER 15

As Misty drove to Owens Security on Monday afternoon, she wondered if she should have given herself more time to recuperate before venturing out. Her head pounded, she felt like someone was punching her in the stomach anytime she attempted to use her core muscles, and her wrist ached. She'd never been one to stay down for long, though, and other than her two trips to the vet, she'd been indoors for almost a week and it was driving her crazy.

When she arrived at the small office on the outskirts of town, Misty walked inside and immediately spotted Walker Owens sitting at his desk in the back office. He'd been very kind to her when he installed her security system about a month ago, and he smiled pleasantly at her now when he swiveled in his desk chair and spotted her.

"Hello, Miss Raven," Walker said as he walked out into the front room. "It's good to see you again. I hope you're still satisfied with your system?"

Misty nodded. "Oh, yes, I certainly am. That's not why I'm here, though. I'm sure you've heard of all the questions I've been asking around town about Elena Himmel and the three girls who disappeared?" When Walker nodded, she continued. "Well, I recently discovered that you coached the girls' volleyball team while Elena taught at the high school. Do you remember her?"

Leaning his elbows onto the front desk, he said, "Yes, I remember her; she taught Spanish. She was very shy and seemed a bit reclusive, and I always wondered if it was because she was self-conscious of her thick accent, or perhaps her husband was the jealous type."

"Do you remember her husband's name?" Misty asked.

Walker shook his head. "No, he was away training a good bit at the military base, and then the Army sent him off somewhere overseas shortly after they moved to Shady Pines." Eyeing her curiously, he tilted his head and said, "You make me think a little of her. She had dark, curly hair just like yours."

Misty's eyes widened in surprise, and she stammered, "R-really? No one has ever said I looked like her."

"Well, you're not identical," he replied, smiling, "but I can see a slight resemblance."

Misty smiled in return, the comment making her feel happy, like she'd stumbled across a missing piece of herself. She'd never had parents or relatives to resemble, and although she still wasn't a hundred percent convinced that Elena Himmel was her mother, hearing Walker's words gave her hope.

"Did she ever mention having a child?" she asked.

Tapping his chin thoughtfully, he said, "I don't remember ever hearing her mention a child, but like I said, we never talked much. My ex wife, however, used to run a nanny service and would probably know if Elena and her husband hired someone to take care of a child."

"That's wonderful!" Misty exclaimed with excitement. "Could I have her number?"

Walker nodded and pulled a business card from his pocket. After jotting down his ex wife's name and number on the back, he handed it to Misty and said with a slight smirk, "Don't tell her I sent you, or you might not get any information out of her. She can be...well, difficult, especially when it comes to me."

Misty took the card and thanked him for his help, and as he returned the pen to his shirt pocket, she caught sight of a bandage on his forearm. Pointing it out, she asked, "Cut yourself on a wire?"

Jerking his gaze downward, Walker quickly pulled his sleeve over the bandage and said, "Yep, happens all the time."

With a smile, Misty thanked him again and waved goodbye. As she got into her car and drove back through town toward home, she spotted Patrick Donovan's restaurant and pulled into an available parking space. Misty hoped Patrick could talk for a moment; it was almost two o'clock, and thankfully the lunch crowd seemed to have died down a bit.

When Misty stepped inside, the receptionist came toward her with a menu, and Misty asked to speak to Patrick.

"He's in his office," the young woman stated, pointing toward a room with a partially opened door. Another customer came in just then, and the receptionist said to Misty, "Why don't you go on back? He won't mind."

Misty had just stepped up to his office when the door swung open and Patrick stepped out. "I heard you asking for me," he greeted her. He wore a crisp, button-down plaid shirt with a solid blue tie, and his thinning dark hair was combed and parted neatly on the side. "How are you, Miss Raven?"

"I'm doing alright," Misty replied. "Do you have a minute?"

"I always have a minute for you, Miss Raven," he said with a charming smile as he motioned for her to step into his office.

As Misty took her seat in the chair across from his desk, she fought off a shiver as images of a dead body lying on this very floor only a few weeks ago flashed through her mind. She hadn't been in this room since, and she pulled her warm sweater tighter around her body like a safety blanket.

"How is your dog, Miss Raven?" Patrick asked as he circled around his desk and sat down.

Shaking off the images in her head, Misty replied, "He's doing better and is back home, safe and sound. How is Mr. Chewie?"

"He's on the mend, thankfully, and as ornery as ever," Patrick chuckled. "So, what can I do for you today?"

Taking a deep breath, Misty decided to just dive right in. "I was told recently that you were the assistant basketball coach at the high school during Elena's time teaching there," she stated in a polite tone. "If you don't mind my asking, why didn't you tell me that when we talked about her before?"

Patrick blinked in surprise and shifted uncomfortably in his seat. "I guess I just didn't think about it," he finally replied with a sheepish shrug. "That was twenty-five years ago, Miss Raven, and I spent the majority of my time teaching over at the elementary school. Surely you can give an old man a break for forgetting a few things."

His last sentence was spoken with a chuckle, and Misty smiled. "Of course," she said. "I spoke with Principal Kirby about possibly going over Elena's records, but he said they recently cleaned out all of their old files. Can you possibly think of another way I can find out more about her?"

His brow furrowing, Patrick tilted his head and said, "I know I don't work there anymore, but the school board was always a stickler about keeping old records, so I can't imagine that Glenn threw them away. Perhaps you should ask his secretary, because I think they're probably still there in the old storage room."

Feeling hopeful, Misty nodded and said, "I'll do that."

There was a knock at Patrick's door just then, and the chef stuck his head in to ask about their cheese vendor. Seeing that Patrick was busy, Misty thanked him for his help and said goodbye.

On her way out, Misty bumped into "Pops" Barlow, Brice and Tori's grandfather, picking up a to-go order. They chatted for a bit, and once he got his order, Misty decided she needed to run to the restroom before heading home. She'd just walked past Patrick's office when she thought she heard her name mentioned, and she stopped to listen at the door.

"I'm sorry I missed your call," he said. "I was talking to Misty Raven; she stopped by to ask some questions about Elena Himmel."

There was a long pause, and then he said, "I know, Catherine, but you shouldn't worry about that. I've already told you I'll take care of it."

Misty blinked in surprise. Was Patrick talking to Catherine O'Reilly?

"Look, she won't find out," Patrick stated, his normally calm tone starting to sound annoyed. "I'll see to that."

Her eyes widening, Misty suddenly caught movement out of the corner of her eye, and she realized with a feeling of panic that someone was about to enter the restaurant. Although Misty was standing in the shadows, she was still in direct view of the front door and would be seen, so she quickly and quietly slipped around the corner and out the back door.

Once in her car, Misty sat there for a moment as thoughts of the conversation she'd just overheard whirled through her mind. What did Patrick and Catherine not want Misty to find out? And whatever it was, did Luxton O'Reilly know as well?

Feeling confused and a little frightened, Misty pulled her car from the parking lot and headed home, deciding not to ask Patrick Donovan anymore questions for a while. His words had felt threatening somehow, and although he'd been nothing but kind to her, Misty suddenly felt the need to stay away from him.

CHAPTER 16

The first thing Misty did the next morning was call the school to ask the secretary about the old records. After doing so, she was placed on hold and waited for over ten minutes until the secretary, Mrs. Benning, finally came back to the phone.

"I'm sorry, but unless you have proof that you're a relative, you can't view any of Elena Himmel's records," she said.

"So…you still have the records?" Misty asked, her eyebrows raising in both surprise and anticipation.

"Yes, of course we do," Mrs. Benning stated impatiently. "Is there anything else I can help you with?"

"No, thank you," Misty replied, and hung up.

Sitting at the kitchen table with a half-eaten omelet on her plate, Misty's mind whirled with thoughts on how she could figure out a way to see those records. Principal Kirby apparently didn't want her looking at them, and instead of simply telling her "no", he'd lied and said they no longer existed. Why? What was in those records that he didn't want Misty to see?

After deliberating for a bit, Misty finally made up her mind; she was going back to that school to confront Glenn Kirby. As she hurriedly finished her breakfast and went to take a shower, she was dismayed to find that her hot water heater had gone out. She immediately called the plumber, and by the time he came out and repaired the hot water heater, school would get out in less than an hour. Still, Misty's mind was made up, so she drove out to the school anyway to speak with Glenn Kirby.

Ten minutes later, Misty arrived at Shady Pines High to find a parking lot full of cars. The school was apparently having some kind of event, so Misty left her car in the park across the street and walked over to the school. No one was around when she entered the front office, and she could hear amplified voices coming from the gym.

"Hello?" she called out, hoping that Mr. Kirby was in his office, but no one responded.

With a frustrated sigh, Misty decided it would be best to come back another day, but just as she turned to go, she spotted a room in the far back corner with "Storage" written above the door. Her eyes widening, she slowly looked around, wondering if she dared go in there. What if someone saw her? Or what if she got in without a problem, but couldn't get out without being seen?

Throwing all caution to the wind and grabbing the chance that presented itself, Misty hurried around the front desk and tried the door handle, her heart picking up speed when it turned easily in her hand. With no hesitation, she quietly slipped inside the dark room and pushed the door back without fully closing it; she wanted to make certain she didn't get locked inside.

The storage room was quite large, with shelves upon shelves of boxes, filing cabinets, and old computers filling most of the space. Not wishing to turn on the lights, Misty pulled out her cellphone and clicked on the flashlight, shining the small beam about the room as she slowly walked around. Each box she passed was labeled with the year of records and files it contained, and as Misty made her way down the aisle that led further and further toward the back of the room, she suddenly heard the sound of voices and approaching footsteps. Her breath catching, she dove behind an old filing cabinet and peered around the side, watching as a shadow fell over the door.

"Isn't our team just the greatest?" a voice spoke out, and Misty immediately recognized it as belonging to Mrs. Benning.

"It certainly is," another, much deeper voice responded. It was none other than Glenn Kirby, and Misty could kick herself for being in the storage room instead of out in the office so she could talk to him.

"It's really amazing how..." Mrs. Benning stopped talking then, and Misty could tell by how close her voice sounded that she was standing just on the other side of the partially opened door. "Now how did this get left opened?" she asked, and Misty's breath stalled. "I'm almost positive I shut this door earlier…oh, well. I guess I only *thought* I shut it."

Her eyes widening with horror, Misty watched as the door slammed shut, and then the lock clicked firmly into place.

She was locked inside.

CHAPTER 17

Misty paced back and forth as panic quickly set in. How was she going to get out? It was almost three o'clock, and everyone would go home soon. She considered beating on the door and calling out, but she could only imagine the trouble she would get in to when they realized she'd been snooping where she didn't belong.

Just stay calm, she tried to convince herself. *Maybe someone will unlock the door before they leave.*

Seizing the time she had in the storage room, Misty clicked on the lights and decided to continue with her search for Elena's records. It took a bit of time, but she finally found the correct set of boxes and eagerly pulled them from the shelf, being careful not to overwork her sore wrist. The boxes were old and dusty, and Misty quickly had to cover a loud sneeze in her sweater, pausing for a moment to make certain no one heard her. When the door remained locked, she opened one box and pulled out a stack of files.

Two hours passed, but Misty barely noticed. She'd gone through every single file in each box twice, but it seemed the year Elena taught at the school wasn't among the rest of the records. It was like the records for that entire year had vanished or simply never existed, but that made little sense because all other years dating back to 1970 were present and accounted for. So why was this particular year, when four women went missing, nowhere to be found?

Feeling both confused and frustrated, Misty put the boxes back and glanced at her watch. When she saw it was nearly 5:30, her eyes widened in dismay. Everyone was probably already gone, and the door to the storage room remained locked. Even if Misty somehow managed to get the door open, it would trigger the alarm and she would be caught before she could make it halfway across the parking lot.

Her stomach rumbling loudly, Misty went to her purse and dug around for her cellphone as an idea took root.

"Since you're a master electrician, you wouldn't happen to have any experience with breaking and entering, would you?"

She sent the text to Adam, and it wasn't long before his reply came through.

"I will neither confirm nor deny that question," he stated with a laughing emoji. *"Why? What are you up to?"*

Misty quickly explained what had happened and told him of her current situation.

"I know it's asking a lot, but can you get me out

138

of here?" she wanted to know.

"I'm still on a job, but I can be there in about forty-five minutes; I'll be the one on the white horse."

Misty laughed, feeling both relieved and a bit guilty that he was going to help her; she only hoped they wouldn't get caught.

After making certain the boxes she'd tampered with were put back into the exact spot they were in originally, Misty began to pace around the room. The minutes crept by agonizingly slow, and she wondered if Adam would ever arrive. Twenty minutes passed, and then thirty, and Misty had just decided to sit down and rest for a bit when she suddenly heard the sound of footsteps. Hurrying to the front of the room, she pressed her ear against the door and listened.

"Yes, I just got back."

The voice clearly belonged to Glenn Kirby, and Misty's eyes widened as panic began setting in once again.

"She called my secretary today and asked about the records again," he said, and Misty immediately knew he was referring to her. "Why did you do that?"

It was apparent that he was talking on the phone, and Misty wondered who was on the other end of the line.

"I *did* get rid of them, but as we both know, if she somehow manages to get her hands on those records, she'll realize that the year she's looking for is missing."

His voice was drawing nearer, and Misty suddenly realized he was heading straight for the storage room. Moving quicker than her aching ribs wanted to allow, she flipped off the light and rushed to hide behind a set of shelves. Her heart pounding, she watched as the lock clicked and the door swung open, revealing Glenn's large silhouette standing in the doorway.

"That's why I've come back to the school tonight," he said, his voice echoing off the linoleum floor as he turned the lights back on. "I want to make sure I didn't miss anything. I'm also going to get rid of several more boxes of old files, so maybe it won't look as obvious."

Misty's heart was pounding so loud, she feared Glenn would hear it as he passed right by her. Thankfully, she was almost completely camouflaged by the boxes that lined the shelves, but what if he happened to peek around the corner and see her standing there? She had to get out of here. When he stopped before the boxes she'd just looked through only minutes before, however, she realized the door was in his direct line of vision, making it almost impossible for her to slip out without being seen.

"Look, all I know is that we need to get rid of her, and soon."

Misty covered a gasp behind one hand, her fingers trembling so badly that she almost scratched her face. Was Glenn the one who tried to kill her at the lake, or the person he was talking to on the phone? Either way, he was obviously dangerous, and she needed to get out of here as quickly as possible before he discovered her.

Slowly and quietly, Misty edged her way toward the door. Thankfully, she'd had the foresight to wear flats, and her footsteps were as light as a feather. Once she reached the end of the shelf, she peered carefully around the corner, fighting back a sigh of frustration when she saw he was facing her. Even though he was staring down at the file he'd pulled from the box, all he would have to do was look up, and Misty knew she couldn't outrun him.

Suddenly, Misty realized Adam would arrive any minute, and her cellphone wasn't on silent. Her heart pounding, she reached into her purse to retrieve her phone, but couldn't find it, and when Glenn said, "Alright, I'll talk to you later," and hung up, leaving the room completely silent, Misty thought her heart would stop entirely.

There! Her fingers finally found her cellphone, and she eased it slowly from her purse and turned the volume all the way down, breathing a sigh of relief when the task was complete. While her phone was out, she sent a quick text to Adam, telling him the situation.

"Don't come inside," she said. *"I'm coming out, so wait for me at the front door with your lights off."*

Without waiting for his reply, Misty replaced her phone and listened as Glenn began to hum under his breath. Peering around the shelf once again, she sighed with relief when she watched him turn slightly away from her to retrieve more files.

Taking a deep breath, Misty headed for the door. Her escape stood only ten to twelve feet away, but it looked as if an ocean rested between them. She'd made it about halfway when, suddenly, a loud clatter echoed throughout the room and Misty froze, her heart nearly coming to a complete stop.

Glancing wildly over her shoulder, Misty saw Glenn lean down to retrieve a box of files that had fallen. Taking the brief second given to her, she quickly took the last few remaining steps that separated her from freedom. She'd just made it through the door and around the corner when a button on her sweater struck the metal doorframe, making a loud and sharp *crack.* Misty paused on the other side of the door and pressed herself against the wall, her heart racing.

"Who's there?" Glenn's voice rang out.

Flinching, Misty could hear his footsteps as he hurriedly walked toward the front office, and she quickly took in her surroundings. The door leading out into the main hallway rested just to her left, and was thankfully standing open. Pushing her trembling legs to move faster than they were willing to go, Misty had barely made it out into the darkened hallway when Glenn stepped from the storage room.

Pressing herself against the wall, Misty clenched her jaw and tried to calm her heavy breathing. The lights from the front office streamed out into the dark hallway, and Misty could see Glenn's shadow growing larger and larger as he walked toward the door. Once he reached the hallway, all he'd have to do was look around the corner and he would see her. What then? If she screamed, would Adam hear her and be able to help in time?

Suddenly, the sound of a cellphone ringing from the storage room broke the silence, causing Misty to jerk. Glenn stopped and, with a sigh, turned and hurried back into the storage room to answer the call. Taking the only chance she had, Misty pushed away from the wall and ran out the front door, her legs weak and trembling. Adam was waiting just around the corner in his car, and she jumped into the passenger seat, completely out of breath.

"L-let's get out of here," she whispered, clutching her aching ribs.

Nodding, Adam pressed his foot against the gas and quickly drove through the dark parking lot.

"Misty, what's going on?" he wanted to know, his brow lowered in concern as he crossed the street and pulled up next to her car.

Leaning her head back against the headrest, Misty took a deep, calming breath and told him everything. Once she'd finished with the story, Adam was staring at her with his mouth open and eyes wide in shock.

"Misty, you've got to tell the police," he told her.

Misty shook her head. "I can't," she replied, sighing. "Not only will they arrest me for trespassing, but it'll be my word against his. I don't have any proof that he said what he did."

"What if the police could check his phone records and see who he was talking to?"

"I'm pretty sure he was using one of those prepaid burner phones," she replied, reaching up to rub her temples. "This is so crazy, Adam. What could Glenn Kirby be hiding in those missing files?"

"I don't know," he stated, running his fingers through his hair. "It makes no sense."

Her head still resting against the seat, Misty looked over at him and said in a tired voice, "I guess I should head home now; I think I've had enough excitement for one night."

Adam reached out and caught her hand as she reached for her purse, his eyes warm as he peered at her through the darkness. "I'm glad you're okay, Misty. As soon as you're back to normal, I plan to teach you self-defense."

Her lips pulling into a grin, Misty said, "That's not such a bad idea, considering the trouble I keep getting myself into."

Leaning across the console, Adam said in a low voice, "Even though I don't mind being the hero who swoops in to save you, Miss Raven, I'd appreciate it if you'd try a little harder to stay out of trouble."

Eyes twinkling, Misty replied, "I can't make any promises, Mr. Dawson, but I'll try."

Their faces were inches apart, and Misty caught

her breath when Adam's eyes drifted down to her lips. Suddenly feeling very warm and flustered, Misty pulled away and, clearing her throat, said, "By the way, thank you for saving me tonight. I'm a little disappointed you didn't come on a white horse, though."

Chuckling, Adam pulled back as well and said, "I'm sorry to disappoint you. *If* there's a next time, and I hope there won't be, I promise to come riding in on my trusty steed."

With a smile, Misty nodded and said goodbye. As she got into her car and drove away, she wondered who Glenn Kirby had been talking to, and why he would have a prepaid phone. Misty was starting to think there were *two* people involved in Elena's disappearance…or her murder.

CHAPTER 18

The next morning, Misty had just sat down to eat breakfast when Adam called. With a smile, she answered the phone with what was to be a cute comment, but he cut her off.

"Have you heard what's happened?"

At the tone in Adam's voice, Misty knew something was terribly wrong. Her body tensing, she said, "No, I haven't. Is everything alright?"

A split second of silence followed her question before Adam replied in a heavy voice, "Glenn Kirby is dead. The school staff found his body in his office this morning. Misty, they're saying it's suicide."

Misty was so shocked that she almost dropped her phone. Making certain she'd heard Adam correctly, she stammered, "He…he's *dead?*"

"Yes. Misty, you haven't told anyone about last night, have you?"

Misty shook her head, even though he couldn't see her. "No, I haven't."

"Good," he replied with a sigh of relief. "Because if anyone finds out you were there, they'll suspect you of being responsible somehow."

"So, you think it wasn't a suicide?" Misty asked, lowering her voice and glancing around as if someone might be listening to their conversation.

"I don't know; it seems like too much of a coincidence to me," Adam stated, and Misty could picture him running his fingers through his hair. "Look, I just arrived at a job, so I've got to go. I just wanted to give you a heads-up, and to warn you not to say anything. Talk to you later?"

Misty agreed, and they hung up. She sat at the table, staring off into space as her mind whirled. Glenn Kirby was dead, and the word was that he'd killed himself...but why were people saying that?

I need more information, she thought, picking up her phone to call Tori. If anyone knew what was being said and why, it would be her.

"Misty, I've been dying to talk to you all morning, but was afraid I'd wake you up," Tori stated in a hurried whisper as soon as she answered the phone. "Have you heard?"

"Yes, Adam just called me. He said it was suicide?"

"That's what people are saying, but the police are still investigating, so I don't know all the details yet," Tori replied, and Misty could hear the noisy chatter of customers in the background. "There was a suicide note, along with some old files or records of some kind. I'm blown away by this, Misty. I've known Glenn Kirby my whole life; he was my teacher, and then later my principal. I can't imagine how poor Kyra must

147

feel!"

Tori's voice broke then, and Misty's heart clenched; if only Tori knew what Misty had overheard last night.

"I'm sorry, Tori," she said gently. "It really is terrible."

"Yeah," Tori sighed. "Look, I'd better go; the shop is packed. I'll call you later, okay?"

As the week progressed, more information on what happened to Glenn Kirby slowly began to surface. When the police arrived at the school and investigated, they found the suicide note and a stack of old files that proved Glenn stole quite a bit of money from the school twenty-five years ago. Apparently, he was head of a committee at the time to oversee several fundraisers to raise money for the school, and with no one's knowledge, he changed the amounts on the records and kept several thousand dollars for himself. If anyone had looked closely at those records, they would have noticed something didn't add up, but Glenn made certain they "disappeared" and no one ever saw them.

To say that the town was in an uproar over this news was an understatement. Some people said they didn't believe it, that their dear high school principal could never have done such a thing, while others speculated on whether his wife, Kyra, had known about it. Misty saw Kyra at the market a few days later, and noticed not only how ragged she looked but also how everyone was staring at her and whispering behind her back. Feeling sorry for the poor woman, Misty made a point to speak and offer her condolences.

With everything that was being said, no one mentioned that Glenn's death may have been anything other than suicide, but after what Misty witnessed at the school, she couldn't help but wonder. Whomever Glenn was talking to on the phone could very well have killed him and made it look like a suicide, and if anyone ever found out Misty was there that night, her life would be in even more danger than before.

CHAPTER 19

That Saturday, six days before Christmas, the town held a Christmas market on Main Street. All of the businesses lining the street set up booths in front of their shops, and Misty offered to help Tori run her booth.

"Are you sure you're feeling up to this?" Tori asked, eyeing her friend with concern as Misty helped carry disposable coffee cups from Tori's shop to the booth.

"Yes, I'm feeling better," Misty replied with a nod. She hadn't told Tori of her little adventure at the school the night that Glenn Kirby died, and even though it was killing her to keep such a secret, she felt it might be too dangerous for her friend to be privy to that information.

Main Street came alive that night as everyone flocked to the market. The town was beautifully decorated with lights, red bows, and Christmas trees. Santa Claus sat on a platform where kids could take pictures with him, while a local band played Christmas music. Visitors from neighboring towns stopped by as well, and soon the street was filled with happy, smiling people with rosy cheeks and twinkling eyes. It was all very magical, and the nip in the air just topped off the heady, exciting feeling that only Christmas can bring.

Tori was the only booth offering hot drinks and baked goods, so everyone stopped at her booth first to buy something warm to eat or drink. Luxton and Catherine O'Reilly's antique booth was just across the street. The drugstore next to Tori's coffee shop was offering handmade soaps and skincare, and the realty company was sponsoring a booth for Jeremy Neely, a local author Misty had met when she first moved to Shady Pines. The other booths offered clothing items, handmade Christmas ornaments, pictures taken by a local photographer, and homemade quilts.

As Misty helped fill the coffee cups and make change for Tori's customers, she couldn't help but notice the way Luxton O'Reilly glared at her every time their eyes met. She hadn't heard from Officer Lewis yet on whether he'd talked to Luxton about his motorcycle or where he was the day she was nearly killed. When she spotted Harlem heading their way, she quickly grabbed the opportunity that presented itself.

"Would you like a brookie with your coffee?" she asked him with a sweet smile when he approached the booth and ordered a cup of black coffee.

His brow furrowing, Officer Lewis asked, "What on earth is a brookie?"

Holding up the individually wrapped bags filled with the delicious treats, Misty said, "It's a brownie and cookie combined. They're delicious; trust me."

Shrugging, Officer Lewis nodded his head in agreement. As Misty took his money and started counting his change, she asked, "I was wondering if you have been able to find out anything about what happened at the lake?"

Officer Lewis took a sip of his coffee and shook his head. "No, I'm afraid not," he replied, his warm breath causing a puff of vapor in the cold night air. "I talked to Luxton O'Reilly, and I was right; he *does* own a black motorcycle, but his wife said he was at the shop with her the morning it happened."

"Did you check the motorcycle for any damage?" Misty asked. "Whoever was driving hit my bike pretty hard."

Cocking an eyebrow at her, Officer Lewis said in a monotone voice, "Yes, Miss Raven, I checked his motorcycle, but there wasn't a scratch on it."

"Doesn't that seem a little odd to you?" Tori spoke up, having apparently overheard their conversation. "Like perhaps he just had it painted?"

At the interruption, Officer Lewis eyed Tori with a slightly annoyed expression. "It could be possible," was all he would say. When both women tried to ask him more, he held up his hand and said, "I'm sorry, but I can't discuss it further.

If I find out anything, Miss Raven, I'll let you know."

After he'd walked off, Tori muttered, "You'd think after everything you did to help solve Cora Griffin's murder, he'd be a little nicer to you."

"I don't think he appreciates my constant interference," Misty replied drolly, instantly becoming distracted when she noticed Adam walking their way with an older couple whom Misty assumed to be his parents.

"Hey, you two," Adam greeted both women with a smile, his eyes especially warm when he looked at Misty. "Misty Raven, I'd like you to meet my parents, Ambrose and Eloise Dawson."

"It sure is nice to meet the girl Adam has been talking so much about," Ambrose stated with a wide smile, exuberantly shaking Misty's hand.

Her cheeks turning red, Misty glanced at Adam to find that he was blushing, as well.

"Ambrose, where are your manners?" Eloise asked with a sigh, giving her husband a firm look. Turning her black eyes that looked so much like her son toward Misty, she said, "It's nice to meet you, Misty. I heard how you helped Officer Lewis solve the Griffin case; that must have been very frightening for you."

As they stood and chatted for a bit about the Griffin case, Misty closely studied the Dawsons, something she always did when meeting someone for the first time. Ambrose was friendly and boisterous, without a shy bone in his body, while

Eloise was the complete opposite. She was polite, but more serious and a bit withdrawn, and Misty found it a little hard to connect with her.

Once the conversation started to die down, Adam spoke up and said, "Well, we're going to see how much Mom can buy tonight, aren't we, Dad?"

Winking at Misty, Adam said he'd text her later, and then waved goodbye to her and Tori. As they walked away, Tori commented, "Well, what do you think of the future in-laws?"

Elbowing her friend, Misty laughed and said, "Stop it. Adam and I aren't dating."

"*Yet,*" Tori stated with a sly smile. "I have to admit that his mom and dad aren't as great as mine, though, and they just happen to be like parents to a certain handsome cousin that I have."

Misty shook her head and sighed. "Don't start that again," she said, rolling her eyes. "Speaking of parents, is Brice's mom coming home for Christmas?"

Tori's expression immediately turned somber, and she shook her head. "No," she replied, sighing. "She was never a great mom to Brice; I honestly don't know why Uncle Barry ever married her, and after he died, she wasn't there for Brice like he needed. When she suddenly married some man she met on the internet and announced she was moving to North Carolina, she and Brice had a terrible argument. They've spoken since then, but she has her own life now and hardly ever comes to visit."

"That's so sad," Misty murmured, her heart

clenching. "Poor Brice."

Just then, Misty's attention was drawn away from her friend and directed at Walker Owens. He was walking down the street with a woman who appeared to be around his age, and it seemed that the two were arguing. Pointing them out to Tori, Misty asked, "Is that Walker Owens' ex wife?"

Tori nodded. "Yeah, it's sad, isn't it? They were married for so many years, and now they're getting a divorce."

"They're not divorced yet?" Misty asked, her brow furrowing. "Because Mr. Owens referred to her as his ex."

"They're separated; I know that much," Tori replied, shrugging.

"Can you make it without me for a few minutes?" Misty asked. "I want to ask her about Elena; Mr. Owens told me she used to run a nanny service."

"Sure, I'll be fine," Tori nodded.

Hurrying down the street after the bickering couple, Misty thought she overheard the words "so long ago" and "why can't you believe me?" before Mr. Owens turned and stalked away from his ex wife, leaving her to stand there glaring after him.

"Mrs. Owens?" Misty called out, lightly touching the woman on the sleeve. When she turned around, Misty saw the anger in her eyes and immediately wondered if she should have waited before approaching her.

"Yes?" she snapped, cocking a well-manicured

eyebrow at Misty.

"I'm sorry to bother you," Misty said with an apologetic smile, "but my name is Misty Raven, and I heard you used to run a nanny service?"

Mrs. Owens stared at Misty for a moment in confusion when, suddenly, her eyes filled with understanding and she said, "Ah, yes, I've heard of you. You're the one looking for your mother, correct?"

Misty nodded. "Yes, Mrs. Owens, that's right."

Her features softening, Mrs. Owens smiled at Misty and said, "You can call me Becca. And, yes, I used to run a nanny service."

The two women walked to one of the nearby shops to get out of the way of the crowd so they could talk, and Misty asked, "Do you remember if Elena Himmel ever used any of your nannies?"

"I do, and she did," Becca replied, and Misty's heart caught. "She had a child; I can't remember if it was a boy or girl, but she asked me if I had anyone Hispanic working for me. I employed one Hispanic lady at the time, a Mrs. Sanchez, and after Mrs. Himmel met with her, she hired her."

"Does Mrs. Sanchez still live in the area?" Misty asked.

Becca hesitated, as if uncertain if she should divulge that information, and Misty all but held her breath as she waited. Finally, Becca said, "I suppose she wouldn't mind if I told you. Mrs. Sanchez lives at 62 Elm Street; she's in her sixties now and her husband died a few years ago, so she would probably love having some company."

Misty touched Becca on the arm and said sincerely, "Thank you *so* much. I've had such a hard time getting anyone to tell me anything, so I'm very excited to have finally found a possible breakthrough."

"I'm happy I could help," Becca replied with a warm smile.

As Becca walked away, Misty stared after her for a moment, feeling a little surprised at how well their conversation had gone. Mr. Owens had insinuated that his wife might be difficult, but as it turned out, she'd been the exact opposite. Perhaps because of the divorce and whatever the two were going through, all he could see at the moment were her faults.

"Penny for your thoughts," a voice said next to her ear, and Misty turned to smile at Brice.

"Surely you can do better than a penny," she teased, her gray eyes sparkling. She wore a green turtleneck dress with a red coat and matching red beret, and her cheeks were flushed from the cold night air.

Tapping his chin mischievously, Brice grinned and said, "Are you sure they're worth more than that?"

Misty punched him playfully on the arm and laughed. "Are you enjoying the market?" she asked as they walked slowly back down the street toward Tori's booth.

"Oh, yes, especially now that I'm about to get a

bag of Tori's molasses cookies," he nodded, his blue eyes wide with excitement.

Her brow furrowing, Misty said, "*If* she has any bags left; they were almost sold out when I was there a few minutes ago."

"Oh, she'll save me a bag," he replied confidently. "She knows how much I love those cookies."

When they arrived back at Tori's booth, Misty had to force herself not to laugh out loud at the look of shock on Brice's face when he discovered Tori had just sold the last bag to her elderly neighbor, Mrs. Ashley.

"She specifically asked for them, and I just couldn't tell her no," Tori explained with a sigh.

"But you could tell *me* no, huh?" Brice huffed, pursing his lips in irritation. Glancing at Misty, he cocked one eyebrow and said drolly, "Here I thought being her cousin gave me extra benefits. Boy, was I wrong."

Misty laughed and shook her head as the two continued to banter back and forth. She returned to her station to keep helping Tori serve her customers, and Brice soon joined Misty in giving out the change.

As the night wore on and the crowd began to dwindle, Misty suddenly felt exhausted. She hadn't realized how busy she would be, and the aching in her stomach and back were telling her she needed to get home and go to bed.

Sensing this, Brice said, "You look tired, Misty.

Why don't you go on home? I'll stay and help Tori clean up."

Tori leaned around her cousin to look at Misty, her face filled with concern. "Oh, Misty, I hope you haven't overdone it tonight," she said.

"I'm just tired," Misty assured them both. Giving Tori a hug, she said, "I had fun helping you tonight. I'll see you at church tomorrow."

Since it was getting so late, Brice offered to walk Misty to her car, and she agreed. As they made their way through the thinning crowd and out to the dark parking lot where the cars belonging to the shop owners were parked, Misty heard raised voices. Peering around the cars, her eyes widened in surprise when she saw Luxton O'Reilly talking to Willow Ruis with his finger pointed in her face. The poor woman was trying to shrink away from the much larger man, her face as white as a ghost, but he grabbed her arm and yanked her back.

"You should have kept your mouth shut, Willow," he was saying, his voice filled with anger. "Haven't I told you that already? Why did you go behind our backs?"

Before Brice and Misty could interfere, another voice called out from the shadows, "That's enough, Luxton. Leave her alone."

Turning, Misty spotted Huey Hendricks hurrying toward Luxton, his jaw clenched. His wife, Darlene, stayed back and watched in silence.

"Stay out of this, Huey," Luxton snapped, his hand still clutching Willow's frail arm in a death grip.

"No, I **won't** stay out of it," Huey shot back, marching up to shove Luxton in the chest. "Let her go right now."

The two men stood nose to nose, and Misty held her breath as she waited for them to come to blows. Luxton released Willow's arm and clenched his hands into tight fists, while Huey continued to stare him dead in the eye without flinching.

"Luxton, please stop this."

It wasn't until then that Misty saw Catherine O'Reilly standing beneath a nearby tree, her eyes red and face dripping with tears. She was staring at her husband pleadingly, and after a moment of hesitation, Luxton stepped away from Huey and stormed off. While Catherine hurried after her husband, Huey turned to ask Willow if she was okay, and Misty could see how badly she was trembling as she nodded "yes" and thanked him.

"Come on, let's get out of here," Brice whispered.

Nodding, Misty followed him to her car, and as they hurried away in the opposite direction, she glanced over her shoulder to see that Darlene Hendricks still stood in the same place, her eyes cold and face set in stone as she silently watched her husband and Willow.

CHAPTER 20

On Monday morning, Misty drove to Elm Street to pay Mrs. Sanchez a visit. As she pulled into the woman's driveway, she felt her stomach clench nervously. Did this woman babysit her when she was a child? If so, would Misty recognize her, or was that just wishful thinking?

Taking a deep breath, Misty climbed from her car and marched up to the front door to ring the bell. In a matter of only a few seconds, a woman in her sixties popped her head around the side of the house, giving Misty a start when she called out.

"Can I help you?" she asked in a thick, Spanish accent.

Blinking in surprise, Misty turned to find Mrs. Sanchez wearing a dirt-covered apron, a silk scarf around her head, and she was holding a hand-shovel in one gloved hand. She was very small, with piercing black eyes and graying black hair, and Misty felt a bit of disappointment when she didn't immediately recognize her.

"Mrs. Sanchez?" Misty asked as she slowly approached the woman.

"Yes?"

"My name is Misty Raven," she stated. "I believe Elena Himmel was my mother. Do…do you remember her? I was told you used to babysit for her."

Mrs. Sanchez studied Misty for a moment, her eyes searching her face as if looking for something familiar, and finally she said, "Yes, I did babysit for her. She was muy encantadora."

At Misty's look of confusion, Mrs. Sanchez smiled and said, "Lovely. Elena was very lovely." Tilting her head, she asked, "If she was your mother, why do you not understand Spanish?"

"Because she abandoned me when I was three."

Misty never enjoyed saying those words. She'd always tried to convince herself there had to be a good reason for her mother to have abandoned her, and the dreams she'd had since she was a child seemed to confirm that. However, what if she was only believing what she wanted to believe? What if her mother simply left because she didn't want her anymore?

"I find it hard to believe that Elena would abandon her child," Mrs. Sanchez stated, her brow furrowed. "She loved her dearly."

Misty caught her breath. "So…so she had a daughter?"

Mrs. Sanchez nodded. "Yes. Her name was Vega, and she was a beautiful child."

"Vega," Misty said softly. "What does that name mean?"

"It means "dweller in the meadow"," she replied,

the words flowing from her lips like a beautiful Spanish song. Stepping closer, Mrs. Sanchez looked into Misty's face, as if she were a gypsy about to tell her fortune. Finally, she smiled gently and said, "Vega had gray eyes, just like you."

Misty struggled not to cry as a flood of emotions washed over her at Mrs. Sanchez's words. She'd been uncertain if Elena really was her mother, but now it seemed to be more real than ever. After so many years of searching, she was finally getting answers. They were trickling in slowly, and a lot of them made little sense, but Misty would keep putting the pieces together until she finally had the truth.

"Mrs. Sanchez," she said in a slightly choked voice, "how did Elena act the last time you saw her? Did she seem frightened or upset?"

Placing the hand-shovel in her apron pocket, Mrs. Sanchez motioned toward her house and asked, "Why don't you come inside and have a cup of Mexican hot chocolate? It's too cold to stand out here for long."

Misty nodded in agreement and followed Mrs. Sanchez into her home. The house was small and very clean, with dozens of photos of Mrs. Sanchez and who Misty assumed must have been her husband. She didn't see any pictures of children, and guessed that Mrs. Sanchez must have loved each of the children she babysat as her own.

After heating a cup of what Mrs. Sanchez explained to be "more spicy and much tastier than regular hot chocolate", she and Misty sat at the table to sip on the delicious drink while they talked.

"The last time I saw Elena, she came home from work around four o'clock, like usual," Mrs. Sanchez stated. Her eyes thoughtful, she said, "She seemed a bit flustered, and I remember noticing that her hands were trembling when she reached out to take Vega from me. I asked if everything was alright and she said it was, so I left."

"Did you think it was strange that she was gone when you returned the next day?"

"That was on a Friday, so I didn't return until the following Monday." Mrs. Sanchez stopped and sighed, a sorrowful look passing over her face. "When I did return, however, there was nothing left. The house had burned to the ground."

Misty's eyes widened in shock. "What happened?" she wanted to know.

Mrs. Sanchez shook her head and shrugged. "I don't know. My husband and I went to Savannah for the weekend, so I had no idea about the fire, but the police suspected it was an electrical fire."

"Was...was there anyone in the house?"

"No," Mrs. Sanchez replied. "No bodies were discovered. When I asked the police where Elena and her daughter were, they said they didn't know. Her car was gone, though, so it appeared she left. There was even talk that she intentionally set fire to the house before running off, but it was never proven and I thought it to be completely absurd."

As Mrs. Sanchez talked, Misty wondered why no one had already told her about this. A mysterious fire followed the disappearance of the high school's Spanish teacher, and no one thought to share that information with her? And in all of her searching and digging through old newspapers, why hadn't she seen something about it?

"Mrs. Sanchez, no one has ever told me about any of this. Do you have any idea why?"

Heaving a sigh, Mrs. Sanchez said, "It was a very strange time for the town. Three local girls had just disappeared, and while everyone wondered about Elena and the fire, no one was overly concerned because she wasn't, well, "one of them". Elena was an outsider, and she preferred to keep it that way."

"Why?" Misty asked, tilting her head.

With a slight, knowing smile, she replied, "When you come from a different country, it's not always easy to adjust and understand the customs. Elena had lived in America for several years and even went to college in Atlanta, but she kept herself distant from everyone and I always got the feeling she'd had a hard life. I even wondered if perhaps she was hiding something, but never asked. I was the closest friend she had in Shady Pines, simply because we were both Spanish and I knew the struggles of moving to a strange country, but we never talked much about personal things."

Misty nodded her head in understanding. "What

about her husband?" she asked. "Do you remember him?"

"Karson? Yes, I remember him," she replied. "He wasn't the friendliest person and was gone a lot, but he seemed to care for Elena."

Karson Himmel. That was Elena's husband's name, and Misty might now know the names of both her parents. It was a breakthrough moment, but Misty tried not to get her hopes up too much just yet. She still had to prove they really *were* her parents.

Misty's cellphone rang just then, and she quickly excused herself when she saw that the call was coming from Officer Lewis. As she hurried into the living room to take the call, she couldn't help but wonder if he would say they'd caught her sneaking out of Shady Pines High on the school's cameras. She'd been nervous about that ever since Friday night, and as she answered the call, her stomach clenched anxiously.

"Miss Raven, I called to tell you that Luxton O'Reilly purchased paint for his motorcycle two days before your accident, so it appears that Miss Barlow's suspicions were correct; his motorcycle *was* recently painted. His wife is still sticking by the alibi, but I'll continue to look in to it."

"Thanks, I appreciate that," Misty said.

"Also, I normally wouldn't discuss this over the phone," he added, "but I'm on my way to see Kyra Kirby and I don't have time to stop by your place first. Before I talk to her, I'd like to know if you spoke with Glenn Kirby the day he died?"

Her heart sinking, Misty cleared her throat and said, "N-no, I didn't. I called the school that day hoping I could talk to him about seeing Elena's records, but his secretary said unless I could prove I was a relative, I couldn't see them."

"I see," was all he said, and Misty got the feeling he was suspicious.

Taking a deep breath, she plunged in and asked, "Why do you ask? Do you think his death wasn't a suicide?"

"I didn't say that," he stated in a clipped tone. "I simply wanted to know if you'd spoken to him."

Knowing she would be found out and probably put in jail if anyone watched those security tapes, Misty found herself asking anyway. That security footage would tell the truth about whether Glenn really was murdered...and who he was talking to on the phone that night.

"Officer Lewis, you know I'm only trying to help when I ask questions like this," she said, her voice trembling just a bit, "but have you checked the school's security cameras from the night he died?"

Officer Lewis sighed heavily, and Misty could picture him rolling his eyes in irritation. "Yes, Miss Raven," he stated drolly, and she felt her body tense. They'd watched the footage? "Or at least we tried to watch it," he added. "Apparently Glenn turned the cameras off when he arrived that night."

Misty blinked in surprise. "Why would he have done that?" she asked.

"I'm guessing so no one would see him shoot himself," he stated bluntly.

Hesitating, Misty asked, "Did you check for gunpowder residue on his hands?"

Officer Lewis didn't answer immediately, and Misty wasn't sure if he was angered by the question or simply surprised. "No, we didn't," he finally said. "Why? Do you think someone killed Glenn Kirby?"

"I don't know," Misty hedged. "It just seems a little suspicious to me. Did y'all check his cellphone?"

"He didn't have his cellphone with him that night, so no, we didn't see any need to check it," he snapped. "Miss Raven, please just stay out of this and let me do my job. Alright?"

"Officer Lewis, I'm only trying to help…"

"Maybe so, but you need to let us handle this," he stated in a firm voice. "Goodbye, Miss Raven."

Harlem hung up, and Misty sat in the living room for a moment in silence, wondering why he was going to see Kyra. She felt guilty for not saying anything about the conversation she'd overheard with Glenn, but she knew for sure now that he was talking on a burner phone that night, a burner phone that couldn't even be found, so there was no way the police could trace the call. She needed to find the killer herself, and she felt in her gut that once she found him or her, she'd also find out what really happened to Elena and those three girls.

With a sigh, Misty stood and made her way back into the kitchen, stopping just outside of the door when she heard Mrs. Sanchez humming a song under her breath as she tidied up the table. The melody was so familiar that it almost took Misty's breath away, and she closed her eyes for a moment, trying to grasp hold of the memory tickling in the back of her mind.

The humming stopped, and Misty opened her eyes to find Mrs. Sanchez watching her curiously.

"What…what was the song you were just singing?" Misty asked, stepping into the room.

With a soft smile, Mrs. Sanchez touched Misty's hand and said, "It's an old Spanish lullaby. I used to sing it to you."

CHAPTER 21

The next few days passed quickly, and Christmas Day dawned bright and cold with a feeling of excitement in the air. Misty was to be at the Barlow's house at noon for Christmas dinner, and she got up early to prepare the Cranberry Fluff she'd offered to bring. She'd learned during Thanksgiving that Mrs. Amy liked to do most of the cooking, but Misty insisted she bring something, and the delightful dish that tasted like dessert but was served with the main course would be the perfect addition.

As she finished up, Misty hummed to the Christmas music playing from her phone and spun around the kitchen, laughing at Wally's curious expression as he watched her from his doggy bed in the corner. He'd sensed her excitement all morning and had eagerly devoured the extra heaping of dog food she'd given him for breakfast. She'd also wrapped a bone for him, and after she placed the Cranberry Fluff in the refrigerator, she called him into the living room to "unwrap" his gift by their fake, two-foot Christmas tree.

As he happily chewed his bone in a corner of the bedroom, Misty jumped into the shower and dressed for dinner. She wore a red A-line skirt, white sweater, and black suede boots, and she pulled her hair up into a high, curly ponytail.

"How do you always know when I'm leaving?" Misty asked Wally when he nudged her with his nose and gave her the ultimate sad puppy-dog look. "I'll be back in a few hours. Make sure you keep your cone on, okay? I don't want to come back to find you've wiggled your way out and chewed your stitches."

He huffed, as if understanding her every word, and she bent over to kiss his nose. Before hurrying out of the house, she grabbed the gifts she'd wrapped for everyone, hoping they would all like what she'd chosen for them.

When Misty arrived at the Barlow's home, everyone was there and the house smelled amazing. She could hear Tori and Mrs. Amy in the kitchen, Christmas music played from a vintage record player in the living room, and the scent of pine needles from the Christmas tree floated in the air, mixing with the aroma of honey-baked ham and yams.

Misty had barely stepped through the door when Brice appeared, looking very handsome in a pair of khaki pants and a brown and navy-blue pullover sweater. As soon as he rounded the corner and saw her, he stopped and his eyes widened as he surveyed her from head to toe.

"Well, Merry Christmas, gorgeous," he stated with a smile as he pulled her into a hug. He took the gifts she was carrying and asked with a wink, "Are these for me?"

As she followed him through the house, Misty laughed and said, "One of them is for you."

Mr. Neil and Pops stood when she entered the living room and gave her a hug, both wishing her a Merry Christmas.

"I'm so glad you could join us," Mr. Neil said, patting her on the back.

Misty thanked them both, and then went into the kitchen to help the women set the table. Mrs. Amy was flustered and frazzled because the ham wasn't quite ready yet, and Misty had to hide her smile when she saw the flour in her hair and a smudge of what appeared to be biscuit dough on her cheek.

"Once I'm finished setting the table, I'm sure it will be ready," Misty assured her.

"This Cranberry Fluff looks so good," Tori told her, eyeing the dish with hungry eyes.

It turned out that Misty was right; as soon as she'd finished setting the table, the ham was done, and it was time to eat. After blessing the food, they all dug in with excitement, and it wasn't long before most of the food was gone and it was time for dessert. Mrs. Amy had made divinity and a red velvet cake with cream cheese frosting, and even though Misty was full from the delicious meal, she couldn't resist trying both of the scrumptious desserts.

As they ate their dessert and sipped on fresh, hot coffee, Misty finally asked the question that had been bugging her all week.

"Do any of you remember Elena's house burning down when she disappeared?"

"I do," Pops nodded.

Looking at him in surprise, Mrs. Amy asked, "Really? I don't remember that at all."

"You'd just had Tori," he replied, "so both you and Neil were a bit preoccupied. I had forgotten about it, though, until just now."

"I haven't seen anything about it in the old newspaper clippings I've been collecting," Misty told him. "Do you have any idea why?"

Leaning back in his chair, Pops crossed one arm over his belly while he rubbed his chin thoughtfully. "If I remember correctly, there was a terrible car accident that night involving our mayor, so I guess the fire just got lost in all the commotion."

"I remember that," Mr. Neil spoke up. "A drunk driver hit Mayor Travers, and he was in the hospital for weeks. It was a pretty big deal."

"Elena's house burned down around the same time she disappeared?" Tori asked Misty.

Misty nodded. "That's what Mrs. Sanchez said," she replied. "She told me the police thought it was an electrical fire, but a few people in town apparently wondered if Elena set it herself before running off."

"I never heard that," Pops stated, pushing his glasses up. "I remember the school board talking about trying to find a new Spanish teacher and how they didn't understand why she left without telling anyone. I don't, however, remember hearing any speculation that she burned her house down."

"She…she wasn't *in* the house when it burned, was she?" Tori asked, her eyes wide.

"Mrs. Sanchez said there were no bodies discovered," Misty replied.

The conversation moved on, and after everyone was finished with their dessert and coffee, they all went into the living room to open presents. The family had already opened most of theirs that morning but had saved a few special ones for Misty's visit, and Misty could hardly contain her excitement as she quickly handed out the gifts she'd brought. She hadn't given anyone a Christmas present since Mr. Sikes passed away, and she nervously waited for everyone to open them.

Brice was the first to tear in to his gift, and he laughed out loud as soon as he saw the huge tin of homemade molasses cookies she'd baked for him.

"I got the recipe from Tori," Misty told him with a grin. "Now Mrs. Ashley can't steal them from you."

"Thank you, Misty," he told her, his blue eyes sparkling as he smiled warmly at her.

Everyone handed Misty a gift, but she simply held them in her lap and watched as they all opened their gifts first. The happiness and joy in the air filled her with a sweet, special feeling she'd never felt before, and she quietly soaked it all in from her seat on the hearth. Tori raved over the friendship music box Misty chose for her, and Mrs. Amy seemed genuinely thrilled with the set of body butter and bath wash from a honey bee store in Savannah.

When Mr. Neil opened his collection of the best old western TV shows, he laughed and said, "This is perfect! Now I can find new names for the three horses I just bought at that auction."

Rolling her eyes, Mrs. Amy said, "I don't think Trampas and Little Joe would appreciate the competition."

With a grin, Mr. Neil leaned over and kissed his wife on the cheek as he said, "On the contrary, dear, I think they'd feel right at home with the addition of a Flint, Marshal Dillon, and Heath Barkley."

"Oh, I always thought Heath Barkley was *so* handsome," Misty stated with a dreamy sigh.

"Us blondes usually are," Brice spoke up, laughing when Tori moaned and punched his arm.

Pops opened his gift next, and Misty watched with hopeful anticipation, feeling relieved when his eyes lit up with pleasure.

"I heard you liked to go fishing on your days off," Misty told him. "So, I thought some new lures would be nice; I hear those are great ones."

Nodding his head in excitement, Pops said, "I've been wanting to try these. Thank you so much, honey."

Everyone hugged and thanked her and then

insisted she open their presents. Feeling both nervous and excited, Misty opened Tori's first, and her mouth dropped open when she saw it was almost exactly the same gift she'd given her.

"I guess great minds think alike," Tori said with a laugh. Her eyes warm, she squeezed Misty's hand and said, "I'm so glad you moved to Shady Pines so we could become friends."

Fighting back tears, Misty nodded in agreement and quickly opened the other gifts. She received a beautiful floral journal from Pops, a Bible from Mrs. Amy and Mr. Neil, and a charm bracelet from Brice with a dog charm that looked just like Wally.

"You're all so thoughtful," Misty told them, feeling a little overwhelmed with emotion as she hugged each of them again. "Thank you all so very much."

After all the gifts were opened, they played a three-team version of Password. Mr. Neil and Mrs. Amy were on a team, Tori and Pops were on another, and Misty and Brice on the third. The game ended up being filled with a lot of fun and laughs, and although they didn't win, Misty was surprised at how well she and Brice played together.

Once it was time to leave, Misty felt sad that the wonderful day was over. Brice and Tori helped load up her car with her gifts and leftover food Mrs. Amy insisted she take, and on the way out for the last time, Brice walked her to the door.

"I'm glad you came today," he said, his eyes

warm as he smiled down at her. "Thank you again for the cookies."

"And thank *you* for the bracelet," she said, touching the delicate chain that was clasped around her wrist. "It's perfect."

"Hey, you two, look!"

Turning, Brice and Misty found Tori standing in the doorway, pointing to something over their heads. Just from the gleam in her friend's eyes, Misty had a feeling that it was mistletoe, and when she slowly raised her head, she saw with a clench of her stomach that she was right.

"You know what that means," Tori stated with a wink.

Her cheeks flushing, Misty glanced at Brice to find him looking a little uncertain as well. "Oh, that's just a silly tradition," Misty stated with a flustered chuckle.

At that moment, the other three members of the family seemed to pop out of nowhere, each with a sly grin on their faces.

"Come on, Brice. What are you waiting for?" Mr. Neil asked, his eyes twinkling.

"You don't have to," Misty told him, feeling very embarrassed and wanting to kill Tori for most likely being responsible for setting this up.

With a slight smile, Brice said softly, "I don't mind."

Blinking in surprise, Misty stood frozen in place as he bent down to kiss her. Just before their lips met, however, her phone suddenly chimed

177

frantically and she jerked away, but not before she saw what looked to be disappointment on Brice's face.

Misty quickly pulled her phone from her purse, her breath catching at the alert flashing across her screen. Raising her eyes to look at Brice, she said in a choked voice, "Someone is breaking into my house."

CHAPTER 22

Just as Misty was hurrying out to her car, the twenty-four-hour operator at Owens Security called her.

"I'm not at home right now, but I'm heading that way," Misty told her.

"We'll have the police meet you there," the lady said.

Brice and Tori hopped into Misty's car with her, while Mr. Neil, Mrs. Amy, and Pops followed behind. As she drove, Misty's whole body was tense and her hands clutched the steering wheel so tightly that her knuckles began to turn white. She knew Wally would try to protect his home, and the thought of someone harming him made her press the gas pedal a little harder.

Misty made it to her house in record time. The police weren't there yet, and as she slammed her car in park and jumped out, she immediately noticed that her front door was standing wide open. Her heart in her throat, she began heading into the house, but Brice quickly grabbed her arm, stopping her.

"We should probably wait for the police," he said, his eyes worried.

"Brice, I don't hear Wally barking," she stated, pulling her arm away. "I'm not waiting for the police; I'm going in now."

All five of the Barlow's followed Misty into the dark house, no one saying a word as she punched a code into her security system to stop it from randomly beeping. Once the system was off, everything became eerily quiet.

Flipping on the foyer light, Misty hurried through the house, calling out for Wally. She'd left him in her bedroom, but that door was open as well, and there was no sign of her dog. There also didn't seem to be any sign of an intruder, but all Misty could focus on was finding Wally.

"I'm going outside to look for him," Misty said as she headed back through the house toward the front door.

"Pops and I will check things out upstairs," Mr. Neil said.

Misty, Brice, Tori, and Mrs. Amy hurried outside, each of them calling out for Wally. With tears pricking the backs of her eyes, Misty headed around the house and puckered her lips, using her special whistle to summon Wally. He knew when he heard that whistle that he was supposed to find her, and she only hoped he'd be able to hear her. What if he'd been let him loose in the woods? She may never find him. Or if someone broke into her house and Wally attacked them, he could be hurt...or worse.

Suddenly, she heard a loud bark, and with a catch

of her breath, Misty saw Wally bounding around the house in search of her. Allowing the tears to flow, Misty kneeled on the ground and wrapped her arms around Wally's neck, burying her face in his fur.

"What happened, buddy?" she asked, leaning back to look at him. His cone was nowhere to be found, and he was covered in dirt and brambles from the woods behind her house.

"He's back here!" Brice called as he hurried their way. "Misty, is he okay?"

"I think so," Misty replied as she gently ran her fingers along Wally's body, searching for any cuts or blood, and sighed with relief when she didn't find any. Standing up, she motioned for Wally to follow her and said, "Come on; let's go inside."

She'd just gotten Wally settled back into her bedroom when an unmarked car with a flashing red light pulled up in front of her house. With a pensive expression, Officer Lewis stepped from the vehicle and walked toward them, and Misty noticed he wasn't wearing his uniform. With a prick of guilt, she realized he must have been at home enjoying the holiday when he was summoned to investigate the break-in.

"Is everyone alright?" he asked, one hand resting lightly on the gun at his side.

Misty nodded. "Yes. I wasn't here when it happened, but got here as quickly as I could."

"Did you see anyone?"

"No, but my front door was open, and someone

181

let my dog out," she replied.

With a frown, Officer Lewis asked, "Was anything taken?"

"Not that we can tell," Mr. Neil stated as he joined them outside, "but Misty hasn't had a chance to go over everything yet."

Pursing his lips, Officer Lewis said, "Well, why don't we do that now?"

Twenty minutes later, Misty concluded that nothing was missing in her house, nor did it appear that any of her belongings had even been touched.

"I think my security system must have scared them away before they could steal anything," she stated as she walked back outside with Officer Lewis.

"I don't think so, Miss Raven," he replied, running his hand over his balding head. "It seems to me that you didn't securely close the front door on your way out this afternoon and your dog pushed it open, triggering the alarm."

Misty thought over what he said and shook her head. "No, I remember locking the front door when I left," she insisted. "And Wally was in my bedroom with the door shut. Surely, he didn't open *two* doors."

With a sigh, Officer Lewis turned to look at her and said, "There's no evidence that anyone tried to break into your home, Miss Raven. I feel confident that this was just one of those weird, random things that happen to us all sometimes. Now, can I please get back to my Christmas dinner?"

Her cheeks flushing, Misty nodded and said, "Yes, of course. I'm sorry to have brought you out for no reason."

Nodding, Officer Lewis marched back to his car without another word and drove away. Misty stood there for a moment, staring after him and feeling rather annoyed as she wondered how he always managed to make her feel so foolish. He didn't believe anyone had broken in, and perhaps he was right, but Misty wasn't convinced. She'd suspected someone had been in her house uninvited only a few days ago, and now she was starting to think that might really be true. Only this time, they hadn't known she'd changed the code on her security system.

"You okay?"

Misty turned to find Brice standing in the doorway, hands in his pockets as he studied her.

"I'm fine," she nodded, crossing her arms. "Just a little frustrated. Why doesn't he ever believe me?"

Moving to stand beside her, Brice sighed and said, "Harlem is known to be difficult sometimes. Plus, he's always had a problem with stubborn, independent women."

Frowning, Misty turned to glare up at Brice. "I am *not* stubborn."

Brice laughed. "Look, I didn't say *I* have a problem with it. In fact," he added with a wink, "I kind of like it."

Misty rolled her eyes and turned away. "Thanks

a lot," she stated drolly. Her mind still on Officer Lewis, she said with a sniff, "I can see why he never married."

"Yeah, he was engaged once, but that ended badly," Brice replied.

Looking at him in surprise, Misty asked, "What happened?"

Brice shrugged. "It was before my time, so all I know is she decided to move to Atlanta and broke it off. Aunt Amy said he was never the same after that."

Frowning, Misty murmured, "How sad."

"So, are you going to be okay here by yourself, or do you want me to stay with you tonight?"

When Misty looked at him in surprise, he chuckled and said, "On the sofa, of course."

"I wouldn't want anyone to have to sleep on that old thing," she snickered. "Thanks for the offer, but I'll be okay. I think whoever it was is scared off for now."

"Well, feel free to call me if you feel even a little uneasy," he said, touching her arm gently. "Promise?"

Misty smiled and nodded. "I promise."

The Barlow's stayed for a little while longer, and when they left, they made her promise to lock all the doors and call them if she needed anything.

As Misty watched their taillights fade away into the distance, she rubbed her arms and shivered, suddenly feeling very alone. She locked the front door and set the alarm system, wondering if she should have taken Brice up on his offer after all.

After Misty fixed Wally's supper, she went into the living room to pack up their little Christmas tree. Although it was still technically the Christmas season, she hated leaving decorations out after the celebrations were over. As she kneeled down to unplug the tree, something on the floor caught her eye. It was half-hidden beneath the sofa, and when she moved closer to investigate, she saw it was a jade earring. She'd seen Kyra Kirby wearing a similar pair when she picked up Wally from the vet two weeks ago, but how had one of Kyra's earrings gotten into Misty's house?

CHAPTER 23

The next morning, Misty called the animal clinic's emergency number, hoping to get up with Kyra Kirby. She not only wanted Kyra to check Wally's foot but also to ask her about the earring.

"I know you're closed for the holiday weekend," she said when Kyra answered the phone, "but I'd feel much better if you could look at Wally's foot. His cone was lost last night during a break-in at my house, and he's tried to lick his foot a few times."

"Someone broke into your home?" Kyra gasped.

"I believe so." Misty quickly explained what had happened, although she suspected Kyra already knew. "Officer Lewis disagrees with me, but I'm not convinced someone wasn't trying to get in."

Kyra agreed to meet Misty at the clinic, and an hour later, Misty pulled into the parking lot and led Wally inside.

"Bring him on back," Kyra said as soon as they walked through the door, and Misty followed her into one of the back rooms.

As Kyra carefully examined Wally's paw, Misty noticed how tired she looked. She was also very quiet, which was unusual for the normally chatty, energetic woman. Perhaps she was just deeply grieving over her husband, and maybe the gossip around town was getting to her.

"How are you doing, Kyra?" Misty asked, breaking the silence between them.

Kyra paused for a brief second and then continued with her examination. "I'm okay. Thank you for asking," she stated, adding in a clipped tone, "You're one of a very few people who've bothered to ask."

"I'm sorry," Misty said. "This has to be very hard on you."

"Yes, it is," Kyra nodded. "What people are saying and how they're treating me is very hurtful."

Misty studied Kyra's profile, taking in her angry expression and the way she clenched her jaw. It almost seemed that Kyra was more upset by what people were saying than over the death of her husband.

"People can definitely surprise you by their actions sometimes," Misty replied. "I heard you had a private funeral."

Kyra made a noise with her mouth, and Misty couldn't tell if it was a mirthless snicker or a frustrated huff.

"Of course I did," she snapped, and Misty drew back at the anger in her voice. "I wasn't about to let my backstabbing "friends" come cry over his casket while offering me fake condolences."

Not knowing what else to say and also seeing the need to change the subject before Kyra tore poor Wally's paw off with her jerky movements as she removed his stitches, Misty cleared her throat and said, "That's a shame; I'm very sorry. So…how does Wally's foot look?"

With a sigh, Kyra stood up straight and pushed her hair away from her face. "It looks good. I removed the stitches, so it may be tender for a few days, but I don't think he'll need another cone."

Sinking back against her chair with relief, Misty smiled and said, "That's great news. Thank you so much for meeting me today, Kyra."

Handing Wally's lead back to Misty, Kyra shrugged and said, "It really was no problem; I needed the distraction, to be honest."

As they walked out into the main room, Misty pulled the jade earring from her pocket and held it out for Kyra to see. "By the way," she said, as if she'd forgotten it was in her pocket, "isn't this your earring, Kyra?"

Her eyes widening slightly, Kyra took the earring and nodded. "Yes, it is," she replied. "Where, uh, did you find it?"

"It was the strangest thing," Misty said, eyeing Kyra closely, "but I found it last night lying under my living room sofa. Do you have any idea how it got there?"

With a slight smile, Kyra put the earring in her pocket and shrugged nonchalantly. "Who knows?" she replied. "I lost it about a week ago. You didn't steal it, did you?"

Kyra ended the question with a laugh, but Misty caught the underhanded accusation. She wondered if Kyra was trying to deflect the attention away from herself by jokingly accusing Misty of stealing the earring. But why would Kyra have broken into her home? None of it made much sense, but Misty knew she couldn't outright accuse the woman of breaking and entering without more evidence.

"No, I didn't steal it," Misty replied in a light tone of voice, "but it's beautiful, so maybe I should have kept it. Finders keepers, you know."

"Glenn gave them to me," Kyra said with a tight smile. "Thanks for returning it to me."

"Thank *you* for healing Wally's paw," Misty said as they walked to the counter so she could pay her final bill. "What made you decide to become a veterinarian?"

"This clinic was first opened by my grandfather over seventy years ago, and then my father took over after him, so I guess being a vet just runs in the family," Kyra replied with a shrug as she booted up her computer. "When my father passed away a few years ago, I wanted to retire, but Glenn…"

Kyra stopped talking and cleared her throat. "Oh, never mind," she continued with a sheepish chuckle, and Misty got the impression she'd almost said too much. "Now that our son is grown and gone, it's nice to have something to do with myself. Especially since I'm now all alone."

"I think it's good for everyone to have something to keep them busy," Misty said as she handed Kyra her credit card.

"Yes, well, you certainly stay busy, don't you?" Kyra asked in an almost sarcastic tone. "How much work is left to do on your house?"

"Oh, I have several more months of work," Misty replied. "The house was in pretty bad shape, and even though I work fast and I'm good at what I do, it's bigger than any other house I've owned."

Clearing her throat, Kyra returned Misty's card and said, "It sounds like you'll be in Shady Pines for a while then before you move on."

Misty blinked. "I'm actually planning to stay in Shady Pines for good."

"But you still haven't found out everything about your past," Kyra stated, her green eyes steady and piercing as she studied Misty. "What if you discover something that leads you away from Shady Pines?"

"I...haven't thought about that," Misty replied, wondering where Kyra was heading with all of this. "I guess I'll cross that bridge when I come to it."

With another tight smile that didn't quite reach her eyes, Kyra nodded and said, "I see. Well, good luck, and just let me know if Wally needs anything."

Misty thanked her and left, and as she walked outside and opened the back door of her car for

Wally, she thought over the odd conversation she'd just had with Kyra. First, the woman seemed hurt and angry over the actions of the townspeople, she then jokingly accused Misty of stealing her earring, and later she acted as if she *wanted* Misty to leave Shady Pines. What happened to the friendly, talkative Kyra Kirby? Misty knew that grief affected people differently, but Kyra's entire demeanor just seemed strange.

After closing the car door behind Wally, Misty walked around to the driver's side and was about to get in when she heard the loud rev of an engine. Spinning, heart in her throat, Misty saw Luxton O'Reilly speeding down Main Street on his black motorcycle. He wasn't wearing a helmet, and his cool blue eyes seemed to look right through her as he passed. She fought off a shiver as she watched him drive by, and just as he turned the corner, she spotted Patrick Donovan stepping out of *O'Reilly's Antiques* with Catherine O'Reilly following close behind. She grabbed his arm and he spun around to say something to her, and although Misty couldn't hear what was being said, it was obvious he was angry. As soon as he finished speaking, he jerked his arm away and got into his car before speeding off in the opposite direction Luxton O'Reilly had just gone.

As Misty watched Catherine wipe her eyes and walk back into the store, she couldn't help but wonder what had just happened.

CHAPTER 24

Sunday morning at church, Adam approached Misty and asked if she'd like to join his family for their annual New Year's Eve celebration. His father, Ambrose, had stopped by her pew to speak when she arrived at the church that morning, while his mother made no attempt to acknowledge her. Misty had bumped into Eloise at the market a few days before, and the small talk they'd both attempted to make was stiff and awkward.

"My parents have a big open house and everyone is invited to come," Adam said, his eyes warm as he spoke.

"Sure, I'd love to come," she agreed with a smile, all the while panicking on the inside as she pictured herself trying to have another one-on-one conversation with his mother.

Stop overthinking this, she told herself. *You'll have a great time.*

Misty had always been an introvert, but the last several years of searching for answers about her past had forced her to come out of her shell and learn to converse with strangers. This shouldn't be any different. Right? So why did she feel so intimidated by Eloise Dawson?

"Great! I'll text you their address," Adam said with a dazzling smile.

"What was that all about?" Tori asked when he walked away.

"He invited me to his family's New Year's Eve party."

Her eyebrows raising, Tori elbowed Misty and said, "Sounds like it's getting serious."

Misty shook her head. "Stop," she said. Pausing briefly, she looked at Tori and asked, "Do many people normally attend, or is it going to be mainly just family?"

Tori shrugged. "I've heard it's normally a pretty big crowd, but I don't really know," she replied. "We always have a family thing, which *you* were going to get invited to, by the way."

"Snooze, you lose," Misty said teasingly.

As she was leaving church, Misty just happened to walk out with the Hendricks'. Giving them both a smile, she asked if they had a good Christmas.

"Yes, our son and his wife came down on Friday; it was just wonderful," Huey said with a bright smile. "Thank you for asking."

Misty blinked in surprise, as she hadn't even realized they had another child. She glanced at Darlene, waiting for her to respond as well, but she never said a word.

"On the night of the Christmas market," Misty stated, "I was heading to my car when Luxton O'Reilly cornered Willow Ruis in the parking lot.

What was that all about?"

Huey shook his head and sighed heavily. "Luxton is a jerk and a bully; he always has been," he stated, stopping to look at his reflection in a nearby car window. After smoothing down his hair and straightening his tie, he added, "Willow has had a lot of issues through the years, and Luxton just saw her as an easy target to take his frustrations out on."

"What sort of frustrations does Luxton have?" Misty asked.

"Why don't you ask Luxton that question?" Darlene spoke up, cocking an eyebrow at Misty.

"He's a bit intimidating," Misty replied with a sheepish shrug. "He paid me a visit, you know, and told me to stop asking questions about what happened to your daughters. Doesn't that seem a little strange to you?"

The air between them suddenly became very tense at Misty's words, and Huey glanced nervously at his wife, who stood in stoic silence with her jaw clenched. Clearing his throat, Huey shrugged and said, "Who knows why Luxton acts the way he does? I honestly don't know how poor Catherine has lived with him all these years."

"Yes, *poor* Catherine," Darlene muttered sarcastically under her breath. With a forced half-smile, she looked at Misty and said, "We'd better get going; I have a chicken in the oven. If you'd like some friendly advice, though, stay away from Luxton. Nothing good ever comes from that man."

Darlene then clasped a firm hand around her husband's arm and pulled him toward their car. As Misty watched them walk away, she wondered what Darlene's "advice" meant. If Luxton O'Reilly really was so dangerous, how had he managed to stay out of jail for so long?

The next morning, Misty called Owens Security to ask if someone could install a couple of cameras outside her house. The woman who answered said Walker Owens would stop by shortly to take a look.

While Misty waited for Walker to arrive, she called the nearby Army base for the third time to try and find out what she could about Karson Himmel. So far, she hadn't had a lot of success, and this time was no exception. She was, however, given an email address to someone who might help her, and as soon as she ended the call, she grabbed her computer and sent the email.

Hardly an hour had passed when Walker Owens arrived at her house, and Misty met him at the front door.

"Why don't you show me where you want the cameras, and I'll get them installed," he said, and Misty nodded in agreement.

"Do you think someone really tried to break in?" he asked as she followed him outside.

Shrugging, Misty replied, "I don't know, but if

they try again, at least I'll have proof this time."

After showing him where she wanted the cameras, Misty sat on the front porch steps as Walker retrieved the cameras and equipment from his truck.

"Did you have a nice Christmas?" she asked him.

"It was…strange," he replied with a half laugh. "Becca and I were married late in life, so we adopted our son, Harold. He always spends Christmas with us, but this year he wanted to reconnect with his birth family, and I also suspect he didn't want to be here while Becca and I are going through a divorce. So, I spent Christmas Eve fishing at the lake, and Christmas Day organizing my new house."

"It sounds like life is a little upside down for you right now," Misty said, watching as he pulled his ladder from the truck bed.

"That's an understatement," he chuckled.

As Walker installed the first camera, Misty held the ladder for him and watched. After a few moments of silence, she was unable to keep her questions at bay. She told him about Luxton O'Reilly's threatening visit to her house and asked his opinion about the man.

"I'm not surprised that he tried to throw his weight around with you," Walker stated, his eyes trained on his work, "but he's harmless. His bark is worse than his bite."

Misty's brow furrowed at that statement. "Darlene Hendricks told me I should probably stay away from him; she sort of gave me the impression that he might be dangerous."

Walker shook his head and chuckled. "Yeah, she's never gotten over the fact that he dumped her back in high school."

"Darlene and Luxton dated?" Misty asked in surprise.

"Yep, for about two years before Catherine started showing him attention," he replied with a nod. "I never understood what Catherine saw in him, but he was one of two guys in our class that she hadn't dated up to that point. I guess she thought she'd add him to her little black book, and then he decided to make their relationship a permanent one."

"Who was the other man Catherine never dated?" Misty asked, tilting her head curiously.

"Patrick Donovan."

At Walker's words, Misty immediately thought of the phone conversation she'd overheard between Patrick and Catherine. Was Patrick the one who got away, and Catherine still wanted him?

"So, she dated you?" Misty asked. When Walker nodded but said nothing, she asked, "What about Glenn Kirby?"

Walker's back stiffened, and he didn't immediately reply. "Yes, she dated Glenn," he finally said. Clearing his throat, he added, "In fact, she dumped me for Glenn."

Misty raised her eyebrows in surprise. "Wow, that must have hurt."

Walker shrugged. "Nah, we were just kids, and it was time we broke up," he replied nonchalantly.

Walker climbed down the ladder then and moved from the front porch to the side of the house, and as Misty followed him, she had the feeling he would prefer she change the subject.

"Mr. Owens," she said once he'd started installing the second camera, "do you use the same code for all of your security systems when you first install them?"

Glancing down at her in surprise, Walker nodded and said, "Yes, I do, which is why I always recommend my clients change it. Why do you ask?"

"I just wondered if whoever tried to break in assumed I never changed it," Misty replied, not bothering to mention that she had no recollection of his ever recommending she change the code. Perhaps he had, and she simply forgot.

"Maybe so, or maybe the front door just blew open," Walker stated.

"Maybe so," Misty muttered.

After Walker finished with his work, Misty paid him and thanked him for coming out so quickly. Once he was gone, she connected the cameras to an app on her phone, already feeling more secure; she wondered why she hadn't thought to do it sooner, but was glad for the extra layer of security the cameras would now provide.

Later, Misty went outside to work on her front porch. Joe Caddel would most likely be delivering her swing and rocking chairs from Cloud Haven soon, and she wanted to be finished with the porch. As she worked, she thought over her conversation with Walker Owens. Was he correct in his statement that Luxton O'Reilly was harmless? She wasn't entirely sure she believed him, but why else had Catherine stayed with him all these years if he really was as horrible as he seemed? Unless she felt she had no other choice but to stay. Misty couldn't imagine being trapped in such a relationship, and hoped Catherine wasn't being abused.

As she pulled nails from all the rotting boards that needed to be replaced, Walker's words about the break-in floated through Misty's mind, and she paused, sitting up straighter. How had he known it was her front door that was left open, and not the back door? Had Officer Lewis told him? Why he would discuss it with Walker Owens, though, Misty didn't know, but she intended to find out.

CHAPTER 25

New Year's Eve arrived, and Misty was thrilled to finish with the front half of the porch that afternoon. She still had the side and back porch to deal with, but at least the front would be ready for the new swing and rocking chairs when they arrived.

Misty put away her tools and dusted herself off before hurrying inside the house. It was time to get ready for the party at Mr. and Mrs. Dawson's house, and she didn't want to be the last one to arrive.

"You're still coming tonight, right?"

Misty had just stepped from the shower when Adam's text came through, and she texted back, *"Coming to what?"*

"Please tell me you're joking," he replied with the face palm emoji.

Misty laughed. *"Yes, I'm still coming tonight,"* she replied with a wink emoji.

After drying her hair, Misty exchanged her bathrobe for a black and white polka dot dress with a knee-length maroon sweater, and then slid into a pair of high-heeled boots. She pulled her hair into a loose chignon, leaving a few curly tendrils hanging around her face, and just before she left, she grabbed the charm bracelet Brice had given her for Christmas and slid it around her wrist.

"It's a good thing we don't have close neighbors," Misty told Wally as she ruffled his ears on her way out. "That way, you won't have to worry about hearing any fireworks."

After entering the address into her phone's GPS, Misty headed for the Dawson's house. By the time she turned down their road, it was a little after eight o'clock, and there wasn't a star in the sky. The night was dark, the road was covered by trees on either side, and Misty had to turn her bright headlights on to better see where she was going. Her phone had just alerted her that the Dawson's home was a little over two miles away when, suddenly, her car made a funny noise.

"What on earth?" she muttered under her breath when her car began to jerk.

Suddenly, a deafening explosion split the air, and Misty clutched the steering wheel as her car jerked wildly to one side. Slamming on the brakes, the car veered to the side of the road, barely missing a tree, before finally coming to a stop.

Misty sat there in silence for a moment, her heart pounding as she wondered what had happened. After a moment, she opened her car door and climbed out on trembling legs, walking around her car with her cellphone's flashlight shining on the tires. When she spotted the flat tire as it still continued spewing out air, she sighed heavily and dialed Adam's number.

"Hey, did you get lost?" he answered, a smile in his voice.

"No, worse," she replied. "One of my tires sprang a leak two miles from your parents' house, and this car doesn't come with a spare."

"I'll be there in five minutes," he said immediately.

She'd just ended the call when the sound of rustling in the woods suddenly met her ears. Turning, Misty peered into the thick, dark trees, her eyes searching the shadows as the rustling drew closer. She immediately assumed it to be some sort of wildlife, but the more she listened, the more she realized it sounded like the footsteps of someone wearing thick, heavy boots instead of an animal.

"Who's there?" she called out, shining the weak flashlight beam over the foliage.

No one answered, but the footsteps stopped, and Misty thought for a moment she'd simply been hearing things. When she shook her head and bent inside the car to retrieve her purse, however, the footsteps started again. Only this time, they were louder and faster.

Her heart in her throat, Misty spun around with the flashlight, ready to confront whoever was out there, when the beam of car headlights suddenly came into view. With a sigh of relief, Misty quickly closed the hood, grabbed her purse, and hurried out to meet Adam as he pulled to a stop in front of her car.

"You okay?" he asked as she quickly climbed into his truck.

"I think I've watched too many scary movies," she said with a nervous laugh as she told him what happened.

Pulling back onto the road, Adam said, "It's deer season, so it might have been a hunter."

"You're probably right," Misty said with a sigh. "I always let my imagination get the best of me."

Adam chuckled. "Well, you've been through a lot lately, so I'd say you have a right to be on edge."

As they rounded the corner, the thick, dark woods disappeared to reveal a large, open area with a beautiful, historic country home right in the center. The house was two stories with a huge wraparound porch and white columns, and golden light glowed from all the windows, lighting up the dark night.

"Oh, this is gorgeous," Misty said dreamily as Adam pulled to a stop. "Is this where you grew up?"

"It sure is," he replied with a nod as he drove around to the back of the house, where everyone was gathered in the barn. Adam parked and walked around the truck to open the door for her, offering his hand as she climbed out. Surveying her from head to toe, he whistled softly and said, "Wow, you look amazing."

Misty blushed. "Thanks," she replied with a

smile. "So do you."

He wore a dark gray, three-button pullover sweater with a pair of denim pants and a light gray coat. He'd freshly shaved, his black hair was smooth and soft, and he smelled amazing. There was no denying that Adam Dawson was a very handsome man; Misty would have to be blind not to see that.

As they walked toward the barn, Misty noted their surroundings. There were approximately thirty people milling about in the beautifully decorated barn, and a huge table of food sat in the corner. Several bonfires flickered and glowed in the field next to the barn, and Misty spotted a few couples walking alongside a small pond. The area was beautiful and peaceful, and Misty wondered how it must have been to be raised in such a place.

As soon as they entered the barn, Misty spotted Adam's parents standing to one side, talking to a young woman with hair as black as Adam's.

"That's my sister," Adam said when he saw where Misty's eyes were directed. "Come on, I'll introduce you."

Misty hadn't realized Adam's sister was in town, and she suddenly felt very nervous about meeting her. As they headed toward Adam's family, Misty smoothed her hands down her dress, hoping Lexi would be friendly like her father.

"Lexi, I'd like you to meet…"

"Wait, let me guess," Lexi interrupted, holding up a hand. Her eyes twinkling, she asked, "Misty?"

Misty smiled and nodded. "That's right. It's nice to meet you, Lexi."

"It's so nice to meet you, too," Lexi replied, stepping forward to give Misty a hug. Pulling back, she gave Misty a once-over and said to her brother, "Adam, you said she was gorgeous, but I didn't expect her to be *this* gorgeous."

Adam laughed. "You just have to see her to believe it."

Misty thanked Lexi for her kind words, relieved to find that she seemed very open and friendly. She was shorter than Misty and very petite, with straight, shoulder-length black hair and a beautiful, dazzling smile.

"I'm glad you could join us tonight, Misty," Adam's mother spoke up, her tone polite. "Adam said your car broke down on the way here?"

Misty nodded. "Yes, ma'am, I have a flat tire," she replied with a sigh.

"Well, Adam will take you home after the party, and I'll get Wallace's number for you; he's our local mechanic," Ambrose, Adam's dad, said. "Just enjoy yourself tonight and don't worry about it."

"Thank you, Mr. Dawson," Misty said with a smile.

A couple of neighbors walked up then, and Adam asked Misty if she'd like something to drink. Nodding, she followed him to the refreshment table, and as he poured a glass of sparkling cider for her, Misty saw Officer Lewis walk in.

"I'm surprised to see him here," Adam stated when he handed her the glass.

"He doesn't normally attend?"

Adam shook his head. "No, not that I can remember."

Just then, Misty spotted the Hendricks' chatting with Patrick Donavon; or at least Darlene was chatting with him. Huey, however, stopped Lexi and appeared to be asking her about Atlanta. As they spoke, his hand kept touching her arm, and Misty noticed Lexi tried backing away from him a few times, but to no avail.

"I'd better go rescue her," Adam murmured to Misty. "She's not very fond of him."

"He seems to be invading her personal space a bit too much," Misty noted.

Adam sighed and nodded. "Yeah, he's always been too friendly with her...and other women, too, for that matter. It makes her uncomfortable."

Misty took a sip of her drink and watched as Adam stepped over and politely interrupted Huey's conversation with his sister.

"Good evening, Miss Raven."

Misty turned to find Officer Lewis standing behind her, and she suddenly realized that she was standing in front of the punch bowl. Moving aside, Misty smiled and nodded.

"Good evening," she replied as he filled his glass. "It's nice to see you here. I'll admit, though, that I expected you to be out chasing down drunk drivers tonight."

With a slight smile, Officer Lewis said, "When you're on the job as long as I've been, you get most holidays off."

"I see," Misty nodded.

Before Misty could think of any annoying questions to badger him with, Adam returned with Lexi in tow.

"Thanks for the rescue," Misty heard Lexi whisper to Adam before she greeted Officer Lewis with a smile. "How are things at the station, Mr. Lewis? I heard that our beloved principal passed away; how tragic."

"Yes, it was," he replied, not bothering to answer her question.

"Have you been able to uncover anything else about his death?" Adam asked, glancing quickly at Misty.

"There was nothing else to uncover," Officer Lewis stated matter-of-factly. "It was pretty obvious what happened when we read the suicide note."

"Was the note typed or handwritten?" Misty heard herself blurt out.

Looking at her curiously, Officer Lewis said, "Typed. Why do you ask?"

Smiling innocently, Misty shrugged and said, "Just curious."

After Officer Lewis walked away, Lexi eyed Adam and Misty closely for a moment. "Why do I get the feeling there's something you're both not telling me about Glenn Kirby's death?" she wanted to know.

"Oh…well, it just seems a little suspicious to me," Adam stated, clearing his throat.

Cocking an eyebrow, Lexi pointed to them both and said, "I've got my eye on you two."

When Lexi walked away, Misty said in a low voice, "Were we that obvious, or is your sister just very perceptive?"

"Perceptive **and** nosy," Adam replied with a chuckle.

Adam's mother approached just then and asked Adam if he'd help her bring more drinks from the house. Adam had just nodded in agreement when his cellphone rang, and with a furrowed brow, he pulled it from his pocket to see who it was.

"This is one of my coworkers," he said. "Give me a minute, Mom."

As Adam walked off to answer the phone call, Eloise sighed and glanced around for someone else to help her, but Ambrose was chatting with the mayor and Lexi was nowhere to be found.

Feeling compelled to offer her services, Misty cleared her throat and said, "I'd be happy to help you, Mrs. Dawson."

Eloise hesitated for a moment before she nodded and said, "Alright. Thank you, Misty."

As they walked towards the house, Misty struggled to find something to say. Eloise didn't try to make any conversation, and the silence between them felt awkward. After a moment,

Misty finally broached the only subject that had been the most relevant to her lately.

"Um, so, Adam told me a while back that you might remember Elena Himmel and the students that disappeared," she said, glancing over at Eloise through the darkness.

"I remember the girls, of course," she replied, nodding slightly. "It was a terrible time for the families. I don't, however, remember Mrs. Himmel."

"I see," Misty muttered as they walked through the back door into a very large kitchen. By the tone in her voice, Eloise didn't seem to want to talk about what happened twenty-five years ago, and Misty would not push her further. Why was it that every time she was around Adam's mother, she felt like the woman didn't like her?

"Here you go," Eloise said, handing Misty a large urn filled with warm apple cider. "If you'll carry this one, I'll grab the hot chocolate."

"Sure," Misty nodded. "This is a beautiful kitchen, by the way."

"Thank you," was all Eloise said as she grabbed the second urn and headed back outside. Misty followed along, not bothering to try to make further conversation. If Eloise wanted to talk to her, then she could broach a subject.

The problem is, I don't think she actually wants to talk to me, Misty thought, sighing inwardly.

"That was such a strange time, when those girls disappeared."

At Eloise's sudden statement, Misty glanced at her in surprise. "I...I'm sure it was," Misty stammered.

"I didn't let my children out of my sight," Eloise continued. "I was terrified something would happen to them."

"I've been told that the girls all left goodbye notes, and the police found no evidence of foul play," Misty said, shifting the urn from one hip to the other.

Eloise sighed and shook her head. "I know, but it just seems so strange to me that three girls would run away from home within just a few months of each other. I know that poor Stephanie Ruis had a good reason to want to run away, but the other two girls certainly didn't. Not that I know of, anyway."

"I heard that one parent hired a private detective, but he never found anything," Misty said.

"That's what everyone was led to believe, but it's not true. They never hired that detective."

CHAPTER 26

Misty stopped walking and put her hand on Eloise's arm, forgetting all about her discomfort as she stared at Adam's mother in surprise. "What do you mean?" she wanted to know.

Glancing around to make sure no one was around, Eloise sighed and said, "I don't like to gossip, but I know you're looking for answers, so please don't repeat what I'm about to tell you."

"I won't tell a soul," Misty promised. "You have my word."

Eloise nodded. "After Jessica disappeared, I went by their house to drop off a crock pot Darlene had loaned me. Darlene's car wasn't there, so I figured I would just leave it with Huey. Right before I knocked on the door, however, I heard his voice drift through the open window. He was talking on the phone to someone; I don't know who, but he said, "yes, I told Darlene I hired the detective, but you should know I don't dare hire one; it would be too risky". I put the crock pot on the door stoop and left without his ever knowing I was there."

Her eyes wide, Misty asked, "Did you tell Darlene?"

"I tried, but she told me I must have misunderstood," Eloise replied. Shaking her head, she added, "Darlene has always been blind when it comes to Huey."

Misty's brow furrowing, she considered everything Eloise had said. "What could Huey want to hide so badly that he wouldn't do everything he could to find his daughter?" she asked, voicing her thoughts out loud.

"Jessica wasn't his daughter."

Blinking, Misty's mouth opened and closed a couple of times before she finally found her voice. "She wasn't Huey's daughter?" she asked.

Eloise shook her head. "Few people know this, but Darlene became pregnant during our senior year in high school. The boy she was dating broke up with her and left Shady Pines, and Huey finally saw his chance to get into one of the wealthiest families in town. He dried her tears and healed her broken heart like the prince charming she'd looked for since her father died, and they were married right before Jessica was born. Most people in town assumed she was Huey's, but I knew better; Darlene and I have been friends since we were in kindergarten."

"Wow," Misty breathed. "Darlene has a lot of money?"

"Yes," Eloise nodded. "Her father left Darlene quite an inheritance when he died."

"Interesting," Misty muttered, her mind swirling. "What could Huey have been hiding that he didn't want a detective to uncover?"

Before they could continue their conversation, Adam stepped outside and spotted them.

"There y'all are," he said as he walked toward them. "I've been looking for you two."

"We were just getting to know each other," Eloise told him, smiling slightly at Misty.

"That's right," Misty said, smiling knowingly in return. "Thank you, Mrs. Dawson."

As the night progressed, Misty tried not to focus on everything Eloise had told her. Instead, she forced herself to relax and enjoy the party. The food was delicious, there was dancing under the barn's string lights, and later, everyone went outside to sit by the bonfire and make s'mores. It seemed that Eloise and Misty had finally found a connection, and the two sat by the fire and talked for a bit while Adam and his father got the fireworks together. Lexi joined them, as well, and the three women laughed and talked about their lives and shared stories from their childhood. It turned out to be a lovely evening, and Misty was glad she came.

"Alright, are you all ready to ring in the new year?" Adam called out.

Everyone nodded and cheered, and after doing the countdown, Adam and Ambrose set off a beautiful display of fireworks. As Misty watched the brilliant flashes of color lighting up the night sky, she found it hard to believe that one year was over and a new one stretched out ahead like an open, unknown road. What would this new year bring? Would she finally find the answers she was looking for?

Once the fireworks were over, Misty insisted she stay around and help clean up, and by the time they were finished, it was after two o'clock and everyone else had already gone home. After bidding the Dawsons a good night, Adam drove Misty home, and Misty heaved a sigh as they drove past her car.

"I hate leaving it here by itself all night," Misty said, covering a yawn as she watched the silhouette of her car fade off into the darkness.

"Do you think it'll get lonely?" Adam teased.

"Hey, it might," Misty replied with a laugh.

Through the dark truck cab, Adam smiled warmly over at Misty, and she smiled back. It seemed they were the only two people in the world just then, and when Adam reached across the console for her hand, Misty didn't pull away. Perhaps it was because she'd had such a good time at the party, or maybe because it was so late and it seemed almost as if they were surrounded within their own intimate cocoon of darkness, but in that moment, Misty felt a certain connection with Adam. She wasn't sure what it all meant and was too tired to think it through just now, so she simply leaned her head back against her seat and listened to the deep rumbles in his voice as he talked about the evening.

By the time they arrived at Misty's house, she was so relaxed that she was nearly asleep. Yawning, she sat up and waited for Adam to walk around the truck to open the door for her.

"I'm glad you came tonight," Adam said as he walked with her to the front door.

"Me, too," she agreed, her heart catching when he interlaced his fingers with hers. "Thanks for inviting me, Adam. I had a great time."

When they reached the front door, Misty realized she'd forgotten to leave the porch light on, and the night was so dark that she could hardly see Adam's face when she looked up at him. She could, however, feel the heat radiating from his body as he stepped closer and touched her chin with his free hand.

"You know," he said, his voice low, "I didn't get a new year's kiss tonight. Did you?"

Misty shook her head, her heart pounding. "No, I didn't."

Through the darkness, she could see Adam's head lowering slowly toward her, and she closed her eyes, waiting to feel the warmth of his lips against hers.

Just when his lips were a mere breath away, a loud *snap* suddenly split through the night, breaking the silence and severing their connection. They pulled away and looked toward the trees that surrounded Misty's house, and her breath caught when Misty saw a shadow move behind the first row of trees.

"Adam, someone is out there," Misty whispered, clutching his arm.

"Who's there?" he called out, his voice echoing through the otherwise silent night. "We see you standing in the trees; show yourself now or I'm calling the police."

Suddenly, the shadow took off at a dead run, and Misty gasped when Adam leaped from the porch in hot pursuit.

"Adam, no!" she cried, afraid that whoever was out there might harm him, but he paid her no heed. Misty watched, her heart pounding, as Adam's silhouette melted into the dark woods, and all she could hear was the crashing of their footsteps.

Instead of doing the wise thing and calling the police, Misty ran after them, her high-heeled boots catching every twig and rock she came across. She could hear Adam calling out as he ran and, suddenly, the revving of an engine joined the chorus of shouts, heavy breathing, and the crunching of dead leaves. Misty skidded to a stop, her heart in her throat as flashes of Lake Laurier popped into her mind, and she listened as the motorcycle gunned its throttle and sped away.

Shaking herself, Misty hurried forward, pushing past branches and stepping over logs as she searched for Adam. She'd just rounded the thick base of a tree when, suddenly, a large shadow loomed before her and she slammed right into a man's chest. With a yelp, she tried to jump back, but two firm hands grasped her by the elbows, leaving her immoveable.

"Misty, are you okay?"

Breathing a sigh of relief when it was Adam's voice she heard, Misty nodded and said, "Y-yes. What happened? Did you see who it was?"

Adam shook his head as they turned and headed back toward the house. "No, I'm afraid not," he replied, his tone heavy. "But whoever it was couldn't have been up to any good. Why else would someone be sneaking around your house this time of night?"

"Adam, the motorcycle sounded exactly like the one that ran me off the road at Lake Laurier," Misty told him, grabbing his hand when she caught her foot on a vine and tripped.

"I don't like this, Misty," he replied, shaking his head. "Someone is stalking you, and we need to put a stop to it. Do you want me to stay with you tonight? Or I can take you back to my parents' place; I know they wouldn't mind if you stayed the with them."

Misty's heart warmed at his show of concern. "That's very sweet, but who knows how long it will take to catch this guy? I can't impose on other people interminably."

They'd reached the porch by then, and Adam pulled Misty to a stop, his hand still holding hers. "It's not an imposition, Misty." His gaze warm, he reached up and gently touched her cheek. "I don't want anything to happen to you."

Smiling softly, Misty said, "Thank you for saying that, Adam, but I'll be fine. I've been on my own pretty much my whole life, so I know how to take care of myself."

"You don't have to be alone anymore," he stated, squeezing her hand. "You have people who care about you now."

Misty swallowed past the sudden lump in her throat as she struggled to find the words to say in response to such a kind statement. How had she gotten so lucky to have stumbled across this town filled with so many people who had welcomed her in with open arms? She'd never felt as if she truly belonged anywhere, but it was different here somehow. In Shady Pines, she felt like she'd returned to her roots, and perhaps she really had.

"I really appreciate that," she finally said, her voice a bit raspy. "It's nice to know I'm not alone anymore."

With a smile, Adam leaned down and kissed her on the cheek. She closed her eyes for a brief second, breathing in the mingled scent of his cologne and smoke from the bonfires that still lingered on his skin. She was coming to care a great deal for Adam, but she wasn't certain if her feelings were of simply friendship or something more. She felt confused and a little dizzy, and when he turned his head toward her lips, she caught her breath and stepped back.

"I-I'd better get inside and see about Wally," she stammered, her cheeks flushing. "Thank you again for everything, Adam."

Nodding, Adam stepped back as well and pushed his hands into his pockets. "I'll wait until you're finished with Wally and have the house secure. Just text me when you're settled, okay?"

Misty promised that she would and hurried inside. Just before she closed the door behind her, she glanced back to see Adam leaning against his truck, patiently waiting. With a small wave, she shut the door, locked it, and leaned against it for a moment as she let out a long, heavy breath. After everything that happened in the last few hours, the only question swirling around in her mind was: ***Am I falling for Adam Dawson?***

CHAPTER 27

When Misty awoke the next morning, she checked her phone and was shocked to find she had a missed call from Father Andrews. He left a voicemail stating he wished to speak with her, but when she called him back, he didn't answer and she realized he'd called from a landline. She mulled it over for a moment until finally making up her mind; she was going to Savannah to look him up. But how would she get there? Her car was still on the Dawson's road. Should she call Adam and ask him to take her to Savannah? Misty was sure he wouldn't mind, but after last night, she wasn't quite ready to face him just yet.

As she thought it over, her phone rang, and she quickly snatched it up to see that it was Tori.

"Hi, Tori," she answered the call, putting it on speakerphone so she could fix Wally's food. "Happy New Year."

"Happy New Year to you, too," Tori replied, and Misty could hear Brice talking in the background. "Do you want to come over to my house? Brice randomly showed up with raw hamburger patties, and I thought we could grill out and play some games or something. You can invite Adam, too, of course."

By the mischievous tone in her voice, Misty could just picture how Tori's blue eyes must be sparkling at her last statement. Shaking her head, Misty told her friend about Father Andrews and her plans to go to Savannah.

"The only problem is that my car broke down, and I have no way of getting there," she said. "Want to bail a friend out and drive me there? I'll pay for the gas, and you can tell Brice to save the burgers for another day."

"That sounds like fun," Tori readily agreed. "We'll be there in fifteen minutes."

As Misty grabbed a banana and hurriedly got dressed, she called "Wallace" to see about getting her car towed and a new tire put on. When the answering service said they were closed until the 2nd, she groaned under her breath and hung up.

I'll just have to leave my car out there until tomorrow, she thought, hoping she wouldn't need it until then.

Tori and Brice arrived shortly, and Misty hopped into the front seat of her friend's car.

"Hey, you two," she greeted them with a smile. "Did y'all have fun last night?"

"We did, but it would have been more fun with you there," Brice stated, reaching up from the back seat to flick her shoulder.

"How was *your* night?" Tori asked, wiggling her eyebrows.

Blushing as memories of her near kiss with Adam floated through her mind, Misty glanced away and cleared her throat awkwardly. "It was very nice," she replied.

Tori looked at her quizzically but didn't say anything, and Brice changed the subject. Before Misty knew it, they were pulling in to the retirement community where Father Andrews lived, and she felt her heart flutter with anxiety.

"I think I should probably go alone," she told her two companions as she unbuckled her seatbelt. "He may be more open to talking if it's just me."

"Good luck," Tori called out as Misty climbed from the car and walked into the front office.

The same lady as before was sitting behind the front desk, and when Misty asked to see Father Andrews, she called his apartment. He answered and told her to let Misty in. Thanking the woman, Misty hurried through the gate and up to his apartment, nervously smoothing down her hair as she knocked on his door and waited.

After a moment, the door swung open and Father Andrews asked her to come inside. Misty followed him through the small but very tidy apartment, sat down on the sofa in the living room, and kindly declined his offer for refreshments.

"Well, Miss Raven, I'm sure you're wondering why I wanted to speak with you," he stated, clearing his throat as he sat across from her. She nodded, her gaze never leaving his, and he tugged at his white collar, as if feeling ill at ease. After a moment, he sighed heavily and said, "I've had you on my mind ever since your first visit. I know I was rude to you, and I'm sorry about that, but I honestly never thought I'd see you again. When you showed up on my doorstep after twenty-five years, it shocked me a great deal."

Misty sat up straighter. "Then…you *do* remember me? And Elena?"

Father Andrews nodded. "Yes, Elena was Catholic, so she came to visit my church often; I sometimes felt as if I was her only friend, and we weren't even that close." Father Andrews stopped and shook his head slightly, his expression thoughtful. "She was a very private person, and I felt that she rarely opened up to anyone. When she showed up at my church that night and asked me to look after you, I was shocked. She seemed so frightened, but wouldn't tell me why, and said she'd be back for you soon."

"So…" Misty stopped and swallowed, finding this all to be a bit surreal, "you really are the man who took me to the police station in Atlanta?"

"Yes," he replied, a look of guilt coming into his eyes. "When Elena didn't return for you after two days, I went to Shady Pines and looked for her. When someone told me she'd disappeared and her house had burned down, I knew that something was dreadfully wrong. I felt that someone was after her the night she left you in my care, and it seemed my suspicions were confirmed." He stopped talking once again and, pulling a white handkerchief from his pocket, he wiped the beads of sweat gathering on his forehead.

"Why didn't you tell the police what my name was?" Misty wanted to know. "And why didn't you tell them of your suspicions?"

"I didn't know what to do," he replied, standing up to pace about the room. "I was afraid that if someone had harmed Elena, they would do the same to you; if that weren't a possibility, why did Elena leave you with me? I was also afraid of becoming involved in a crime; my parish was already crumbling, and I didn't want to lose everything I'd worked so hard for. So, I took you to that police station and told them I didn't know your name. I did it for your protection…and my own. I hope you can forgive me."

Father Andrews bowed his head in shame, and even though Misty had a right to be angry with him, she couldn't seem to find any anger in her heart. He'd done what he thought was best at the time, and for all either of them knew, he may have even saved her life.

"Of course, I forgive you," she said gently. "I can now say I know for certain that Elena Himmel really was my mother, and for that, I thank you."

His eyes brimming with tears, Father Andrews raised his head and looked at Misty. "Thank you, Miss Raven…or should I say, Miss Himmel?"

Misty smiled. "No. I'll always be Misty Raven." Tilting her head thoughtfully, she asked, "Do you remember seeing anyone that night, Father

Andrews?"

Father Andrews sat back down and thought over the question for a moment. "I didn't see anyone that night," he finally replied, "but I remember her mentioning once about her students going missing and how she didn't think they really ran away. She even said that she'd noticed something a little strange at the school a few times, and when I asked her what, she wouldn't tell me; all she would say was that if someone looked close enough, they'd possibly find the truth. Do you think that had something to do with her disappearance?"

Misty nodded her head slowly. "Yes, I do," she said. "I'm not sure how it all ties in together, but somehow I get the feeling the disappearance of those girls and my mother are connected. Did Elena ever mention anyone's name from Shady Pines?"

"The only people she ever talked about were her husband and a Mrs. Sanchez," he replied. "But like I said, she shared little of her personal life."

Nodding, Misty stood up and offered her hand to Father Andrews. "Well, I won't take anymore of your time. If you should happen to remember anything else, please give me a call." Gently squeezing his hand, she smiled and said, "Thank you so much for everything, Father Andrews. I can't tell you how much I appreciate it."

Father Andrews patted the back of her hand and said, "You're very welcome. God bless you, Miss Raven. And don't give up; sometimes we find what we're looking for in the most unexpected places."

Thanking him once again, Misty said goodbye and left. As she walked down the apartment building stairs, she felt tears pricking the back of her eyes. Elena Himmel really was her mother; she knew that for certain now and felt overwhelmed with emotions. How could something so precious, so personal, be confirmed by a total stranger? If life had been normal, she would have already *known* Elena Himmel was her mother, because Elena would have raised her, loved her, soothed away her hurts and fears, and taught her things that only a mother can teach. Instead, Misty had been robbed of it all. Would she ever know what really happened? Elena could still be alive, and Misty may never discover the truth. And what about her father? Did Karson come home, looking for his wife and daughter, only to find they'd both disappeared into thin air? Did he even search for them?

Needing a moment to herself to clear her mind, Misty sat on the bottom step and closed her eyes, taking a few deep breaths. She wanted to be happy that she was finally finding answers, but all she could do was cry. Had she really expected this to be easy? No, she'd known the truth would most likely be hard, but she'd still had hope of finding something positive.

If I never know what happened to my mother, at least I still have a slight chance of tracking down my father, she told herself. She wanted to find her family, and maybe someone at the army base would help her.

Feeling a little better, Misty wiped her face and stood up, making certain to keep her shoulders tall. She wouldn't let this pull her down; there was still hope.

"How did it go?" Tori and Brice asked simultaneously when Misty got into the car.

Heaving a sigh, Misty told them everything, and she couldn't help but smile when they both tried their best to encourage her.

"At least you know for certain now who your parents are," Tori said, reaching out to squeeze Misty's hand. "That's more than you've ever known."

"You'll get there, Misty," Brice spoke up from the back seat. "If you keep trying, I know you'll find all the answers. You've already uncovered something most people in your circumstances never could, so don't give up."

"Thanks, y'all," Misty said, smiling at them both. "Now, let's go have some fun."

Putting her car in reverse, Tori backed out of the parking space and said, "I want to do some shopping on Broughton Street, and before we head home, I want to swing by Baker's Pride."

Misty's forehead wrinkled as she glanced over at her friend. "I've never heard of that," she said.

With a dramatic sigh and a look of pleasure filling her face, Tori said, "They have the ***best*** chocolate chewy cookies you've ever tasted!"

"*And* donuts," Brice piped in. "They're in midtown Savannah, over where the hospitals are located."

They spent the rest of the day shopping on Broughton Street, eating on the rooftop of a restaurant on River Street, and walking along the cobblestone streets beneath the towering oaks. When it was time to go home, they stopped by Baker's Pride on their way out, and Misty discovered that Tori was right; they *did* make the best chocolate chewy cookies she'd ever tasted. As they drove back home, laughing and talking and eating sweets from the bakery, Misty felt more thankful than ever for her friendship with the delightful Barlow cousins. If not for them, her day would have been much more grim.

CHAPTER 28

That evening, after Brice and Tori left, Misty sat at the kitchen table, eating another cookie and thinking about the conversation with Father Andrews. Something he'd said kept repeating itself over and over in her mind: ***"Elena said she'd noticed something a little strange at the school a few times, and when I asked her what, she wouldn't tell me; all she would say was that if someone looked close enough, they'd possibly find the truth."***

By all accounts, Elena was a very quiet, private person, and most often the quiet ones were the most observant. Whatever she'd seen must not have been very obvious to other people, and she'd told Father Andrews that one simply had to look close enough.

With an idea tickling the back of her mind, Misty swallowed the last bite of her cookie and walked to her bedroom where she retrieved the yearbook Willow Ruis had given her. Sitting cross-legged on her bed, Misty slowly looked through the book once again. She carefully studied each photograph, trying to find something she might have missed before; she even grabbed her old magnifying glass to get a closer look at a few of the pictures. Nothing was jumping out at her, and when she reached the last page, she sighed heavily and started to close the book. Just before it shut, the last page fluttered over, and Misty realized the back two pages were filled with signatures and little handwritten notes. She casually glanced through them, smiling at the silly notes left by typical teenagers, but when she came to one particular note and signature, she paused, her brow furrowing as she read the note.

"You know what you did. -Puffy" was written very small in the bottom, right-hand corner. Misty studied it for a moment, wondering what it meant. It could have simply been a harmless note written by one of Stephanie's classmates, but the message somehow seemed different from the others. Was Misty reading more into this than was necessary, or did the message mean something more? And who was "Puffy"?

After debating with herself for a moment, Misty decided to pay Willow Ruis a visit and ask her about it. She wasn't sure why, but this message meant something; she could feel it.

The next morning, Misty called Wallace once again and was finally able to get her car towed to his shop. After working a few hours on the house, Misty received a call from him, informing her that her car was ready.

"I don't know what caused your tire to go flat, Miss Raven," he told her. "It almost looks like someone cut it lightly enough that the air wouldn't seep out until you were driving, but that's just ridiculous."

Misty told him she'd be there to pick up her car shortly and then called Tori to ask if she could pick her up. Tori agreed, and while Misty waited, she thought over what the mechanic said. Had someone purposefully cut her tire? Just then, she remembered the sound of footsteps she'd heard out in the woods after her tire went flat; had someone planned to attack her while she was stranded on that dark, lonely road, but was interrupted when Adam arrived? Shivering, Misty rubbed her arms, thankful that Adam showed up when he did.

Tori arrived shortly and dropped Misty off at the mechanic shop, where Misty paid the man and thanked him for getting her car fixed so quickly. Ten minutes later, she pulled up in front of Willow Ruis' house, hoping the woman was home.

Misty approached the small, slightly run-down house and knocked on the front door, the yearbook clutched against her chest as she waited. A dog barked loudly from inside the house, and a moment later, the door opened and Willow peered out, her translucent colored eyes lighting up with recognition when she saw Misty.

"Miss Raven," she said in that same light, airy voice, "how nice to see you. Please, come in."

Misty followed her into the living room, apologizing for showing up uninvited. "What kind of dog do you have?" she asked as she sat down on the stained, lumpy sofa.

"Oh, she's just an old mutt I've had for years," Willow replied with a shrug. "She hasn't been acting right, though, so I'm worried she's getting sick."

"I'm sorry to hear that," Misty said. "I hope she'll be okay." An awkward moment of silence filled the air then, and holding up the yearbook, Misty explained, "The reason I stopped by is that I saw something in Stephanie's yearbook I wanted to ask you about."

"Oh…would you like something to drink first?" Willow asked, wringing her hands uncertainly, as if she wasn't accustomed to having visitors.

Misty smiled and shook her head. "No, thank you."

Nodding, Willow came to sit beside Misty, tucking a strand of stringy brown hair behind one ear. Misty opened the yearbook to the last page and was just about to point out the strange note when, suddenly, the dog started barking again just before the doorbell rang. Her brow furrowing, Willow excused herself and got up to hurry back through the house.

Misty sat and waited, listening as Willow opened the front door. As soon as Willow said, "Hey, Puffy, you didn't have to come by today," Misty's eyes widened and she stood up, her heart racing.

Walking slowly through the living room and into the foyer, Misty leaned around to see who was at the front door.

"Hello, Miss Raven," the one called "Puffy" said. "I didn't realize you had company, Willow."

Willow turned to look at Misty and said, "Yes, Misty stopped by to…"

"Oh, it's not important," Misty interrupted with a wave of her hand. Clearing her throat, she looked at Willow's visitor and asked, "Did…did I just hear Willow call you Puffy?"

Puffy sighed. "Yes, when I was young, everyone accused me of having a puffed up opinion of myself, so I guess the nickname just stuck. I wish no one would use it now, though," Puffy added with a disapproving glance at Willow. "We're too old for nicknames."

Biting her lower lip, Willow said softly, "I'm sorry."

Turning to look at Misty, Puffy's eyes drifted downward to stare at the yearbook she clutched in her hands, and Misty fought the urge to hide it behind her back. With a nervous smile, Misty said, "Well, I'd better get going. I'll see you later, Willow."

With a look of confusion, Willow asked, "But I thought you wanted to show me something in Stephanie's old yearbook?"

"Maybe later," Misty said, quickly skirting around Willow's visitor as she hurried out the door. Once she made it to her car, she turned to find Puffy still standing in the doorway, watching her with piercing eyes.

As Misty drove away from Willow's house, she tried to decide what to do. Should she go to the police and tell them of her suspicions? No, she didn't have any proof, and they'd just think she'd lost her mind. She needed to get home and go back through everything to try to put the pieces together.

Fifteen minutes later, Misty was in her bedroom pouring over the old newspaper clippings she'd collected in the last eight years. Something had struck her as odd when she'd gone over them the last time, and now she had a feeling she knew what it was. As she studied over them, her eyes widened as memories of a certain conversation floated through her mind, and she placed several of the articles in a separate pile. She then opened the yearbook once again and flipped through the pages until she came across a certain picture. Grabbing her magnifying glass, she drew the photo in closer and nodded when she found what she was looking for. It had been there all along; she just hadn't been able to see it until now.

Glancing at her watch, Misty's eyes widened when she realized that two hours had passed. Was it too late in the day to go to the police station with everything she'd uncovered? Jumping from her bed, she closed Wally up in the bedroom and was heading toward the kitchen to get something to drink when her doorbell rang. Sighing, Misty changed directions and made her way through the house and into the foyer. Her mind was so filled with everything she'd just discovered that she didn't think twice about opening her front door without first asking who it was, but as soon as she did so, her breath caught and she choked back a gasp.

There, standing on her front porch, was Kyra Kirby, and she was aiming a gun directly at Misty's face.

CHAPTER 29

Kyra, what are you doing?" Misty asked, her heart kicking into overdrive.

"Don't play games with me, Miss Raven," Kyra said. There were swollen, dark circles around her eyes, as if she hadn't slept in days, and her red hair was a mess. "Just step inside the house."

Misty slowly backed away, keeping her hands up and eyes trained on Kyra. Her mind whirled as she tried to figure out how she could knock the gun out of Kyra's hand without getting herself killed, and she suddenly wished she hadn't locked Wally in the bedroom.

"Why are you doing this, Kyra?" Misty asked, hoping to keep Kyra talking while she figured out what to do.

"You were at the school that night," Kyra snapped, her green eyes flashing. "The night Glenn died."

Misty blinked in surprise. "How…how did you find that out?" she asked as they came to a standstill in the living room.

"You were caught entering the school on the cameras," Kyra stated, her jaw clenching, "and you didn't leave until after Glenn turned them off that evening. Why did you kill my husband? Would he not tell you more about your precious mother?"

Misty's eyes had been slowly moving around the room, searching for something she could use as a weapon, but her gaze jerked back to Kyra's at the woman's question.

"What are you talking about?" Misty asked, her brow furrowing in confusion. "I didn't kill Glenn, Kyra."

A look of confusion passed over Kyra's face as well, but was quickly replaced with anger as she clenched the gun tighter and hissed, "Stop trying to distract me!"

"I'm not," Misty insisted. "You're right. I was there that night, but I didn't kill your husband. He was talking on the phone to someone about possibly killing *me,* but I don't know who it was, and I sneaked out of there as quickly as I could. He never even knew I was there."

Kyra studied her with a look of suspicion, the gun lowering slightly. "I...I don't know who he could have been talking to, because there were no recent calls on his cellphone," she stated, her voice wavering uncertainly.

"He was talking on a burner phone," Misty told her. "I could see it through the shelves I was hiding behind."

Kyra's eyes filled with tears, and she reached up to rub her temple. "I'm so confused," she whispered, shaking her head.

Just then, Misty saw a shadow moving through the foyer, and her heart caught. Was someone there to help her? Squinting her eyes, she watched as the shadow drew closer and then slowly stepped into the light.

"Officer Lewis," Misty breathed.

Kyra spun around, the gun waving through the air toward the policeman. Holding up his hands, Officer Lewis said, "Don't shoot, Kyra."

"What are you doing here?" Kyra demanded, her voice trembling.

"I stopped by to speak with Miss Raven about why she was at the school the night your husband died," he replied, eyeing Kyra's gun uncertainly. She still clutched it tightly in her white fingers, and the gun wavered back and forth between Misty and Harlem as she watched them both with a crazed expression.

"We both know that's not why you're here, Officer Lewis," Misty stated. "Or should I say, "Puffy"?"

With a slight smirk pulling at his lips, Officer Lewis turned to look at Misty and said in a slow, even tone, "You're right, it's not. I knew you'd figured it out when I saw you at Willow's house this afternoon, which is why I had to put my plan into action immediately."

Looking back and forth between them, Kyra asked, "What's going on? What are you two talking about?"

"Officer Lewis here, also known as "Puffy", killed your husband, Kyra, along with those three high school girls twenty-five years ago," Misty said. Staring at Officer Lewis, she asked, "Did you also kill Elena?"

"She found out about my little secret, so of course I had to kill her," he replied, and Misty noticed he was slowly inching toward Kyra. "Glenn suspected I was involved, and when he threatened to go to the police, I said I'd tell everyone about the money I knew he'd stolen. So, he kept my secret for all these years. When you started poking around, though, he got nervous, and I was afraid he'd break down and tell everything he knew, so I had to get rid of him, too."

"*You* killed my husband?" Kyra gasped.

Looking at Kyra with a sneer, Officer Lewis shrugged and said, "I had no other choice."

With a scream, Kyra raised the gun upward and lunged at Harlem, her hair flying wildly around her face, but he was too quick for her. Before Misty could even blink, Harlem disarmed Kyra and shoved her roughly to the floor, aiming the gun into her face.

"I have cameras outside, Harlem," Misty suddenly spoke up, desperately trying to divert his attention. "If you kill us, they'll know it was you."

Sighing, Officer Lewis looked at Misty and raised an eyebrow. "You underestimate me, Miss Raven. I know you have cameras, which is why I told Kyra you killed her husband. She's been asking a lot of questions since Glenn died and I knew she suspected foul play, so I set this little meeting up on purpose. I plan to tell the police that Kyra had just killed you when I stopped by and interrupted. When she turned her gun on me, I was forced to defend myself. The fact that she brought her own gun, which I'm sure will be visible in the camera footage, is just icing on the cake."

Officer Lewis slowly pulled the hammer back on the gun, and Misty quickly blurted out, "Those three girls and Elena weren't the only ones, were they, Harlem? You've been killing girls all over Georgia for years."

Glancing back at Misty, a look of surprise passed Harlem's face before he laughed. "I should have known you'd figure that out, too. Ever the nosy little amateur detective, aren't you?"

"The night Cora Griffin was killed, you told me you were in Savannah," Misty said. "When I looked through my old newspaper clippings, I saw where a young woman disappeared that weekend. How many women have you killed, Harlem? And why?"

Misty could hear Wally scratching at the bedroom door, and when Harlem hesitated, as if trying to decide whether to explain or go ahead and kill the two women, she scrambled to come up with a plan. Harlem was standing between Misty and the front door; if she ran out the back door, there was nowhere to go except into the woods, and she didn't want to repeat that nightmare scenario again. Her car keys were in the foyer, her cellphone was in the bedroom, and Harlem had a gun. How was she going to get out of this alive?

"It-it's because of Terri, isn't it?" Kyra spoke up, her trembling voice breaking the silence.

Misty looked at her in confusion and then raised her eyes to search Harlem's face. His jaw was clenched tight, and Misty saw a bit of sweat forming on his brow.

"Don't mention her name," he hissed, and Misty's eyes widened slightly. Whoever Terri was, just mentioning her name was causing the calm and calculated detective to lose his cool.

"Was Terri your fiancé?" Misty asked.

"Yes, she was Stephanie Ruis' aunt," Kyra said, eyeing Harlem cautiously. "She and Harlem were engaged until…"

"Until she decided to dump me and move to Atlanta," Officer Lewis snapped, his face turning red.

"So, you killed her niece to get back at her?" Misty asked.

"Of course not," he stated, shaking his head. "Stephanie came on to me after Terri and I broke up. She told me she'd always had a crush on me, so we started having a secret affair."

"Which was easy since you worked part time at the school as an SRO," Misty said, shaking her head in disbelief. "I saw a picture in the yearbook of Stephanie with a man I thought was Walker Owens, but when I discovered you were "Puffy",

I looked again and realized it was you."

Harlem nodded, his lips curling with satisfaction. "Once again, you're correct, Miss Raven. Stephanie was crazy about me, and it was hard to keep it a secret from her friends, but I convinced her it was for the best."

"Did you plan to kill her all along?" Misty wanted to know.

"No," he stated coldly. "I was just using Stephanie, but when she started pressuring me to marry her, I told her it wasn't going to happen and she threatened to get me arrested for having a relationship with a minor. So, I convinced her to write the goodbye note and meet me secretly so we could run away together." Pausing, Harlem smirked and added, "She never pressured me again after that."

"Why kill the other girls, though?" Misty asked, suddenly catching sight of a hammer she'd left lying on the back of the sofa from the corner of her eye. If she could slowly ease herself in that direction, maybe she could use it as a weapon. Keeping her eyes trained on Harlem, she began inching to her left, her heart pounding.

Chuckling, Harlem lowered the gun slightly and said in an arrogant tone, "Because it was fun, Miss Raven. You can't possibly understand the thrill of playing such a dangerous game. I was young and good-looking, and all of those stupid girls threw themselves at me. It was so easy! And once I grew tired of them, I'd execute the trickiest part of it all;

I'd convince them to leave their home and run away with me. It worked every time. There's just something about a man in uniform, you know."

"But you decided to broaden your horizons when Elena discovered what you were doing," Misty said. "It got a little too dangerous to keep playing that game in such a small town."

"Exactly." Raising the gun to point it at Misty, Harlem said, "First I had to get rid of Elena, and now it's her daughter's turn. Ironic, isn't it?"

Misty's heart stopped, and she stood frozen in place as she watched his finger slowly begin to squeeze the trigger. She told herself to move, to make a run for the hammer, but couldn't seem to force herself into action. It was like time paused and everything moved in slow motion. Harlem killed her mother; now he would kill her.

Just before the gun fired, Kyra threw herself into Harlem's legs, throwing him off balance, and Misty felt the whir of the bullet as it flew directly by her head. Snapping out of the trance she was in, Misty launched across the living room and grabbed the hammer, her fingers trembling so badly that she almost dropped it. Spinning back around, she saw Harlem hit Kyra on the head with the gun, and watched in horror as the veterinarian slumped to the floor, a pool of blood quickly forming around her temple.

With adrenaline pumping through her veins, Misty lunged across the space that separated them and kicked the gun from Harlem's hand. It clattered across the wooden floor, and as Misty moved to grab it, Harlem gripped her around the ankle and sent her spiraling downward. She hit the hard wood with a grunt, but before she could turn over to defend herself, Harlem grabbed her by the hair and yanked her roughly back up.

Misty screamed, fear flooding over her when she realized she'd lost her only chance to survive. She could hear Wally barking and pounding on the bedroom door with his paws, and she hoped Harlem wouldn't kill him, too, if he escaped.

His hand gripped her forearm painfully as Harlem snatched the gun off the floor and pressed it against her temple. "You're a fighter, just like your stupid mother," he hissed into her ear. "You both should have just minded your own business."

As soon as those words were uttered from his lips, anger like she'd never known before coursed over Misty's body with a burning, raging heat. With a cry that could rival that of a tribal warrior, she slammed her head into his nose with a satisfying *crack.*

Grunting, Harlem released her arm and stumbled backward, giving her only but a second to grab the hammer from the floor, spin around, and swing it at the gun. She made contact, and the gun went flying across the room. Before she could rear back again and strike Harlem, however, his hands were suddenly around her neck. Struggling with all her might, Misty tried to break free from her assailant, but he was too strong for her. Stars floated before her eyes, her ears were ringing, and her lungs screamed for air. Was this the end? Had Harlem won? All she could think about was her mother, and how she'd done everything she could to protect her. Just before she blacked out, a sudden memory floated through her mind. Misty could clearly see her mother handing her over to Father Andrews that dark night so long ago. There were tears in Elena's beautiful eyes and a look of pure agony on her face as she walked away from her crying daughter and out of the church doors, and a sob caught in Misty's chest as the life began fading from her body.

Suddenly, the sound of a door crashing against the wall split the silence, and Misty could hear the pounding of Wally's paws as he ran down the hall toward the living room. With a fierce growl, Wally appeared from around the corner and lunged at Harlem, knocking him away from Misty and onto the ground. Gasping for air, Misty stumbled back against the wall and sank to the floor, her legs too weak to hold her weight, and she watched with a pounding heart as man and dog fought.

I have to do something, Misty told herself. With a deep breath of determination, she pushed herself to her knees and crawled toward the gun, her head swimming and stomach rolling. Wally could easily tear Harlem to pieces, but if Harlem somehow got the upper hand, he would kill Wally and then finish what he'd come for.

Her fingers found the gun, and with a grunt,

Misty turned and pointed it at Harlem.

"Wally, stop," she commanded, uncertain if her dog would obey, but he quickly released his master's attacker and moved to stand beside her.

Harlem slowly turned his head to look at her, his clothes torn and blood dripping from the wounds at his neck, and when their eyes met, Misty pulled back the hammer on the gun.

"It's been twenty-five years since you killed my mother," she said, her voice trembling but firm. "I'd say it's high time you paid for what you did. Don't you, Puffy?"

CHAPTER 30

With Wally standing guard at her side, Misty managed to rouse Kyra up and told her to call 911. Both women were exhausted and weak, and when Misty finally heard the sound of approaching sirens, she breathed a sigh of relief. It was finally over.

Officer Dylan Mitchell, Harlem's partner, didn't want to believe Misty or Kyra when they explained what happened, but when Misty told him she could match Harlem's visits to various cities where young women had disappeared over the last twenty-five years, he finally agreed to take him into custody while it was all being investigated. Misty suspected they would find evidence at Harlem's house once it was searched and knew without a doubt that after the investigation was complete, Officer Harlem Lewis would never again be a free man.

After they'd taken Harlem away, one paramedic was trying to talk Misty into going to the hospital when she heard a familiar voice calling her name. Turning, she saw Adam hurrying through the house with a look of alarm on his handsome face.

"Misty, are you alright?" he asked, coming to

stand at her side.

"Yes," Misty nodded with a small smile. "But how did you know what happened?"

"I didn't," he replied. "I still don't know what's going on; I just haven't heard from you in a few days, so I thought I'd stop by and see how you're doing. What's going on?"

"Well, to make a long story short, Harlem Lewis is the murderer who killed those three girls and Elena…my mother…twenty-five years ago."

Hearing her own words hit Misty like a ton of bricks, and she swayed slightly on her feet. Adam grabbed her arm and led her to the sofa, but she shook her head and whispered, "I need to get out of here, Adam. Please, take me some place away from these prying eyes where I can fall apart, and I want Wally to come along."

After receiving clearance to leave the crime scene, Adam drove Misty and Wally away from the house. Misty told him where she wanted to go and then quietly leaned her head back against the seat, her eyes trained on the side mirror as she watched her house and everything that had happened there fade into the distance. She was weak and sore and probably needed to go to the hospital, but all she wanted was some peace and quiet so she could process everything.

Reaching through the silence that separated them, Adam took Misty's hand and continued to drive. Ten minutes later, he turned down a dirt road and stopped before an empty field. Giving him a smile of thanks, Misty climbed from the truck and got Wally out of the back so he could go with her. They walked down what used to be the driveway and stopped to stand before the foundation that still rested in its original location. Looking around, Misty felt a pang of sadness that she had no memories of ever being here before, but things were much different from the last time she was here.

This is the place where Misty, Elena, and Karson lived for a short period before everything fell apart. The foundation before her was the charred remains of the house that held...what? Love, laughter, sadness? Misty couldn't remember, and as she stood looking out at the land that now belonged to a farmer, tears filled her eyes and she sank to her knees and began to cry. She cried for the life lost to her, for parents she could barely remember, and for a mother who fought so hard to save her daughter. If only Misty could see her one more time, she would thank her and tell her how much she loved and missed her.

A wet, furry nose nudged Misty's cheek then, and with a watery smile, she put her arms around her dog's neck and squeezed him tightly.

"Thank you," she whispered. "You saved my life, you know. I had no idea how lucky I would be when Tori showed up with you on my doorstep, but I'm sure glad she did."

The two of them sat there for a few moments longer when Misty heard Adam's truck door shut and then the sound of his approaching footsteps. Standing to her feet, she wiped her face and turned to look at him.

"Are you alright?" he asked, gently reaching up to touch her cheek. His beautiful black eyes were filled with concern, and his familiar scent was so comforting to Misty at that moment.

"Yes," she nodded, smiling. "Thank you for bringing me here." Taking a deep breath, Misty let it out slowly as she turned to once more survey the land that surrounded them. "It's been a long eight years," she said softly, "but I'm glad I finally have the answers I've been looking for."

"Do...do you think you'll be able to stay after everything that's happened?" Adam asked hesitantly.

Misty thought it over for a moment before she finally nodded and said, "This is my home now, Adam. I wouldn't want to live anywhere else."

The sun was setting when they made their way back to his truck, hand in hand. Adam put Wally in the back and fastened his leash, and when he came to open the passenger side door for Misty, his face was full of shadows, but she could feel the warmth in his eyes as he stared down at her.

"You know," he said, one hand on the door handle and the other resting on her arm, "now that you've found your answers, I'd say it's time for you to settle down with someone and start dating."

Her lips twitching, Misty raised her eyebrows and asked, "Oh? Do you have anyone in particular in mind?"

"Yes," he replied, a grin slowly spreading across his face. "As a matter of fact, I do."

Running his hand lightly up her arm until his fingers rested along the side of her face, Adam leaned over and pressed his lips against hers. Misty's eyes fluttered closed, and she stepped closer to him, soaking in the feeling of his warmth and strength as she wrapped her arms around his waist and returned his kiss with a fervency she hadn't felt in years. Yes, she'd finally found her home, and she knew now that her feelings for Adam ran much deeper than friendship. She didn't know where it would lead, but she was finally willing to give it a try.

Over the next two weeks, more and more evidence began coming to light as the police investigated Officer Harlem Lewis and the disappearance of the three high school girls. Misty and Kyra had to give their full statements down at the station, and all the parents were questioned once again about their daughters. Through the rumor mill, Misty discovered that Huey Hendricks never hired the private detective because he didn't want the fact that he was having an affair with Catherine O'Reilly to come to light. He knew if Darlene found out, she'd file for divorce and leave him penniless, so he simply ended the affair and lied to his wife about the detective. Luxton O'Reilly also knew about the affair, which is why he'd tried to stop Misty from asking too many questions by coming to her house that morning and threatening her. It was, however, Harlem who tried to kill her with a black motorcycle no one knew he owned.

After searching Harlem's house, the police uncovered a box filled with "souvenirs" from all the women he'd killed. It was more than enough for a conviction, and all anyone in town could talk about was how shocked they were. How was it that another murderer, and one of their very own law enforcement officers no less, had lived among them for all these years and no one suspected a thing? It seems you never really know a person.

With Harlem behind bars and her past finally filled with answers, Misty was able to go back to her bed-and-breakfast with a feeling of peace and closure. A lot had happened in that old house, but it only seemed to make Misty feel more determined than ever to bring new life and new beginnings back into it. This was her home now, and she wouldn't have it any other way.

EPILOGUE

One month later

Misty stood before the small, one story brick house, her heart fluttering nervously within her chest as she tucked a stray curl behind one ear. Two days ago, she'd received an email regarding her father, Karson Himmel. It was from his mother, and she'd asked Misty to come see her at her home just outside of Jacksonville, Florida.

"I was told you've been searching for him," she wrote, *"and I'd like to see you in person. There is a lot we need to discuss."*

Mrs. Himmel seemed very direct and to the point in her email, and not at all excited to have found her long lost granddaughter. Could she possibly think Misty was lying, or was Misty overthinking again?

Taking a deep breath, Misty walked to the front door and knocked, her heart kicking into overdrive when the door opened only a few seconds later. There, standing before her, was Karson Himmel's mother. Misty's grandmother.

Swallowing past the lump in her throat, Misty said, "Hello, Mrs. Himmel. I'm Misty Raven."

"Please, come in," Mrs. Himmel said, her face set in stone as she stepped aside to allow Misty entrance.

They went into the living room and sat on the sofa, and Misty nervously smoothed her skirt down over her knees. There were several pictures lining the mantle, and when Misty spotted a photo of a young man in uniform, she caught her breath and felt tears spring into her eyes. It had to be Karson, and Misty studied the picture closely, searching for any resemblance they might share. He was blonde, with a fair complexion and wide set blue eyes, and he had a stern expression that matched his mother's. His jaw was firm, and Misty noticed a small scar on his right cheek.

"I'd offer you refreshments, but I think we would both like to just get to the point," Mrs. Himmel stated, bringing Misty's attention away from the picture. "I was told that you know nothing about Karson. Is that correct?"

Misty nodded, feeling very intimidated by the small, stern lady who sat beside her. "That's right," she replied. "I recently discovered that Elena Himmel was my mother, and she was killed twenty-five years ago when Karson was away on deployment. I was hoping to find him, but had just about given up hope when I received your email. Does…does he live here in Jacksonville?"

Mrs. Himmel sighed and shook her head. "No, Miss Raven," she said, her eyes filling with sadness. "My son was killed in an explosion during the deployment you just mentioned."

Misty stared at Mrs. Himmel in shock, her heart sinking down into her stomach like a lead balloon. Her father was dead, too? A sob caught in her throat, and Misty put her hand to her mouth and tried to force it back. She didn't want to break down and cry in front of this woman, but the sudden pain was almost more than she could bear. She'd hoped that at least one of her parents would still be alive, but now knew with a feeling of despair that she really was an orphan after all.

"I-I'm sorry for your loss, Mrs. Himmel," Misty finally said in a broken whisper. Shaking herself, she cleared her throat and asked, "Would you mind telling me where my father is buried? I'd like to visit his grave before I leave."

Looking a bit uncomfortable, Mrs. Himmel shifted in her seat and said hesitantly, "That's the reason I wanted to see you in person, Miss Raven. You see, Elena was already pregnant when Karson met her. I'm sorry, but my son was not your father."

A NOTE FROM THE AUTHOR

Thank you so much for reading book #2 of "A Shady Pines Mystery" series. Now on to book #3, *Storms of the Past*! If you enjoyed it, please leave a review on Amazon or Goodreads – or both! I look forward to hearing from you. Also, if you're interested in receiving news of upcoming books, discounts, free e-books, and more, please sign up for my newsletter at: https://newsletter.jennyelaineauthor.com/

Storms of the Past
A Shady Pines Mystery, Book 3

"Legend has it that when the black wolf is spotted, death is sure to follow."

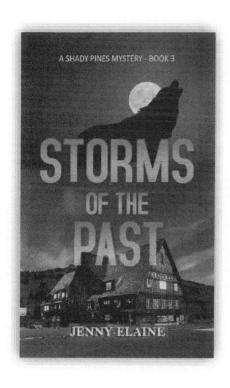

Years ago, in the hills of North Georgia, the Indians told a story of a lone black wolf that emerged from the smoke of revenge. The story became a legend, and now when the wolf is seen, it is said that someone will die. After learning her mother once lived in Dahlonega, Misty travels to Black Wolf Lodge in search of answers. While there, a deadly storm sweeps through the mountains, ravaging the area and trapping everyone at the lodge. When one of the guests is killed, the legend of the black wolf is blamed, but Misty feels there could be a murderer lurking in their midst. As she delves into the secrets of the lodge, buried truths come to light and mysteries of the past are finally revealed.

THE HEALING ROSE OF SAVANNAH

ROSE OF SAVANNAH SERIES – BOOK 1

While seeking solace from a broken heart, Savannah Rose travels to the picturesque city of Savannah, Georgia, only to find herself trapped within the confines of romance, murder, and mystery. It is the 1940's, a war is being waged in Europe, and a serial killer stalks the streets of Savannah, targeting young women and terrorizing the city. When the killer sets his sights on Savannah Rose, she must fight to survive, and in an attempt to save her life, she journeys away from the city only to encounter tragedy and more heartbreak. Forced to return home and face the danger that continues to lurk among the shadows, Savannah Rose struggles to overcome the obstacles thrown into her path. Along the way, she searches for healing, discovers the real meaning of life, and finds her one true love. Blended with rich history and creative storytelling, this suspenseful saga sweeps readers back and forth between the 1940's and the 1960's,and will keep you captivated until its final conclusion.

"What a wonderful book. It kept my attention the whole time and I had no clue of how it would end, until the last page!! Thoroughly enjoyed it!"
-Goodreads review

"This is an amazing story full of mystery, romance, and suspense. It was such a great read, I could hardly put it down!"
-Goodreads review

"A very good and moving story line. Enjoyed the book and the history. Some laughs and tears. Good read for a raining day."
-Amazon review

"Loved this book! Enjoyed the shift between '40's & 60s'. This story had it all: mystery, romance, humor, sorrow, a prominent family's secret and twists I never saw coming. I hated to see it end and wish a sequel was in the works."
-Amazon review

THE WHISPERING SHADOWS OF SAVANNAH

ROSE OF SAVANNAH SERIES – BOOK 2

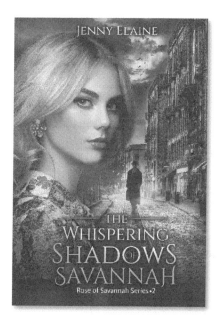

It is the 1940s, and Vivian McCombs witnesses a horrible crime on the outskirts of Savannah, Georgia. When no one will believe her story, she is accused of being responsible for the crime and sent away. Desperate to prove her innocence, Vivian is forced to endure the chaos that has overtaken her life. Upon her return home three months later, Vivian befriends Eva Beckett, a young immigrant who is struggling to support her family after the death of her husband. When strange things begin to occur, both women must fight to conquer the dangers that lurk among the whispering shadows.

Follow the lives of these two brave women as they form friendships, search for healing, gather strength to overcome life's obstacles, and find love along the way. The alluring history of Savannah will captivate you in this astounding story of mystery, courage, romance, and suspense.

"A wonderful 2nd book in this series. It was attention-grabbing from the beginning! I found it hard to put down and read it from cover to cover within about 6 hours."
-Amazon Review

"Once again, I was blown away by the author and her ability to write such captivating, real-life moments and do it in a way that left me breathless. It was incredibly well-written and impossible not to picture the scenes playing out as I read along."
-Amazon Review

"Great read!! I thoroughly enjoyed this book. If you like romance, mystery, and historical fiction you will love this book."
-Goodreads Review

Made in the USA
Middletown, DE
23 July 2023